ELi
OVER
EASY

Also by Phil Stamper

Small Town Pride

PHIL STAMPER

ELi OVER EASY

HARPER

An Imprint of HarperCollinsPublishers

Library of Congress Control Number: 2023934232
ISBN 978-0-06-311883-6

Typography by David Curtis
23 24 25 26 27 LBC 5 4 3 2 1

First Edition

To Blake Addison,
with all my love.

1

```
<!DOCTYPE HTML>
<HTML>
    <HEAD>
        ELI OVER EASY
    </HEAD>
    <BODY>
        <P>I MISS YOU</P>
    </BODY>
</HTML>
```

Dad won't stop pacing around my bedroom. I watch him take a few steps toward my bookshelf, then to my small desk, and finally back to the foot of my bed, all while rambling about the importance of keeping the front door locked while he's at work. He repeats this action, silently this time—thank goodness—so I close my eyes and try to squeeze in a few more milliseconds of sleep.

It's *way* too early for this.

"Mrs. Martinez is right next door," he says, as if we haven't gone over this before. As if I don't know where our literal neighbor lives. "She'll come and check on you this afternoon, but if anyone knocks on the door, what do we do?"

1

"We get the step stool out and look through the peephole before letting anyone in." I pull the covers over my head in a weak attempt to end the convo.

"Right." He takes a sharp breath. "Just like at the old house."

This apartment is nothing like the old house, I think. But I don't dare say it aloud. The move to our tiny Manhattan apartment only took a couple days, but the last six months have been a hard adjustment, to say the least. Mom led the charge, though, despite my dad's hesitation, and before I knew it, we *were* adjusted.

But a few months ago, Mom died, which makes us . . . whatever the opposite of adjusted is. De-adjusted? Un-adjusted? Falling apart. A piece of broken computer code, full of bugs I can't find.

"I'm going to be fine," I tell my dad after he takes another lap around my tiny room. I lower my voice to sound a little more confident. "I'm thirteen."

He takes a seat at the foot of my bed and pats my leg, staring off in the distance.

"I just can't believe they're making me go into the office full time now." He sighs. "Eli, I'm going to find a new job where we can go back to Minneapolis—back *home*—I promise. Until then, just promise you won't leave this apartment, so I know you're safe."

"I won't—"

"—unless you hear a fire alarm," he interrupts. "Then you find Mrs. Martinez and—"

"There's *not* going to be a fire alarm," I say confidently. "It's fine, Dad. Just go to work."

He stands again, after a bit of hesitation, and paces another lap around the bed.

"Get up," he says, exhaustion weighing down his voice. "I'll walk you through all the emergency numbers on the fridge."

I roll out of bed after a slightly melodramatic sigh and follow him into the main area of our apartment, a teeny-tiny space that the living room *and* the kitchen somehow fit into. *Gotta love New York City!* A list on the fridge has phone numbers of everything from hospitals to Poison Control to the superintendent of the building. It also has all the account information for all of Dad's restaurant delivery apps. He walks me through them in excruciating detail.

He's been a little bit like this ever since we moved to New York City, but since Mom died, his anxiety has gotten worse. He's hesitant, repetitive, frazzled, uncomfortable.

As he grabs his messenger bag and opens the door, I remind myself that it'll get better someday. It *has* to.

"Love you, Eli," he finally says.

With the kindest smile I can muster in this tired state, I push him into the hallway. "Love you too."

I shut the door with a sigh. Before I can even turn the deadlock from my end, Dad uses the key to lock it, then checks the knob in case it somehow didn't work. I groan.

The remnants of last night's dinner are strewn all through the apartment, from the coffee table to the kitchen island to the counters by the sink, so I go around and collect the garbage. Since we moved, one thing we learned the hard way was that if you leave garbage out in an apartment for too long, some critter *will* find it.

No one told me that moving to a Manhattan apartment means starting a never-ending battle with cockroaches. *Yuck.*

Once the apartment is straightened up, a brief sense of calm comes over me . . . but that calm quickly turns into loneliness. I step into the kitchen to look for some breakfast, but I lose my appetite when I see the picture

4

of me, Mom, and Dad on the fridge. My shoulders cave in some, and I feel the energy draining from my body as a few unwelcome tears prick at my eyes.

I've been left alone plenty, but this time feels different. Dad's been so overprotective since Mom died three months ago that this sudden freedom, knowing I have eight hours to myself while Dad's in the office, feels immediately overwhelming. I feel a grief spiral coming on, so I quickly FaceTime my cousin Riley, in the hopes that she's awake.

The call connects immediately.

"Eli! How's my favorite cousin?" she says with a laugh. Even though it's eight in the morning in Minnesota, she's looking perky as ever. She runs a hand through her long black hair, showing off a new bright pink streak she debuted for her stream last week. Her face is literally glowing, her pale skin harshly lit from one of the many ring lights that make up her bedroom-slash-video-game-streaming-studio.

"You're up early," I say, ducking out of sight to find a hat to cover my messy hair. She's already camera ready, and I look like I just rolled out of bed . . . which I did. "Wasn't sure you'd answer."

"The new *Songbird Hollow* expansion just came out, and I'm obsessed," she says while touching up her makeup in her bedroom mirror, "so I'll be live streaming the game all morning. You should check it out."

I nod vacantly, as I always do when she talks about video games and streaming. Though it's never been my thing, she's built up a pretty good following of fellow video game nerds who watch her play. Ever since we moved here, having her streams on makes me feel a little less alone, even if I have no idea what she's talking about half the time.

"How are you doing?" she asks while arranging a series of plushies to go in the background of her stream. "Did your dad actually go to work today?"

"He did," I say, willing some sense of independence to come back to me. But then I deflate. "I feel very . . . alone right now."

She stops what she's doing and turns to look at me. "Need to talk about it?"

"No, it's fine, you're busy. I could just feel myself spiraling and wanted to see a friendly face." I shake my head. "My virtual summer coding boot camp starts soon, but I'll keep your stream up on the TV. Between my new classmates and you—and all your adoring fans, of course—how could I be lonely?"

"Exactly." She smirks. "I can't believe the first thing you do after school ends is . . . sign up for more school. What a nerd."

"I think we're both pretty nerdy."

"Terminally nerdy," she says with a laugh. "Isn't it the best?"

I root through the fridge and freezer for the third time since I started the call, eventually sighing when I realize there's nothing I want to eat. It's all frozen breakfast burritos and other microwavable egg dishes. *Gross.*

I plonk a burrito on a plate and throw it in the microwave, then set it for two minutes.

"What's for breakfast?" Riley asks, and I shake my head.

"What else? A breakfast burrito that will somehow be both scalding hot and ice cold at the same time. It's magical, really."

"Ooh, remember those breakfast burritos your mom used to make? Where she'd put the hash browns *in* the burrito? Oh, or those little Hungarian crepe things?"

"Palacsinta," I say, and for a brief moment, I'm missing more than just Mom's cooking. The questionable

7

smell of the burrito clashes with the memory of the amazing smells that used to come out of this kitchen.

Mom's passion for cooking is the thing that brought us to New York City in the first place. She got a job in the test kitchen for a big food magazine, creating and perfecting recipes so they could publish them. But when she came home, she'd cook one of her own staples. Chicken paprikash, fried bread, and so many other dishes I'll never have again. I take a deep breath to keep the tears at bay.

"Sorry," she says weakly. "I'm sure this burrito will be good too."

I shrug. "It is what it is."

There's a silence that comes over us, one that I'd normally want to patch up with distracting talk about something, anything, but I don't have the energy for it.

"I've got to go," I say after a few more seconds. "Good luck on your stream today. I'll tune in, promise."

"No, you focus on your coding class! You've been begging to go to this academy for *years*. Aren't you so excited?"

"I am!" I say, though I know my face doesn't show it. "Just feeling weird today. But you're right, I've been wanting to do this boot camp forever. Did I tell you we're going to fully design and code our own app by the end of the summer?"

"That's so cool," she says. "You're going to crush it, trust me."

I smile and say goodbye before ending the FaceTime. I take my piping-hot burrito from the microwave, throw it on a plate, grab a bottle of hot sauce, and walk into the living room.

I try to focus on my upcoming coding class. I've been waiting for this for so long, and I've been practicing too, spending countless hours on websites with free coding activities. With some logic and a few lines of code, you can tell a computer to do anything.

Hope swells in my chest, but as soon as I bite into the bland frozen burrito, burning the roof of my mouth, that hope dies. The dam breaks, and the first tear falls.

Having a professional cook as a mom came with a ton of benefits, even if the test kitchen kept her working late most days. When she died, I knew it would be hard, and that I'd have reminders of her all around . . . but this is too much.

Every time I microwave a lackluster burrito, I think of what I've lost.

My coding class doesn't start for another forty-five

minutes, so I take my breakfast to bed and curl into the covers as I eat. Halfway through the burrito, I set the plate on my nightstand and slide fully under the blanket. I set an alarm for five minutes before the class starts and try not to think of her as I drift off back to sleep.

2

```
<!DOCTYPE HTML>
<HTML>
    <HEAD>
        ELI OVER EASY
    </HEAD>
    <BODY>
        <P>I MISS YOU</P>
    </BODY>
</HTML>
```

I wake up a few minutes before my alarm, thanks to a "just checking in! everything ok?" text from my dad. I groan and make my way back to the living room so I can get into coding mode.

Okay, this is when the excitement hits, I think. But as I open Mom's laptop, sign into our online course portal, and start pulling up instructional videos and waiting for the Zoom session to start, the emptiness inside me holds on.

I glance through the syllabus, and as I look in more detail at our final projects, our weekly videos and coding activities, finally some bit of adrenaline floods through me. It's a little overwhelming, but I know I can do it.

As a kid, I'd beg Dad to find me different logic puzzles,

sudoku, math problems. He couldn't keep up, until his developer coworker suggested something that might interest me: coding. And I haven't looked back since.

My brain eases as I pull up a lo-fi music track on YouTube and put on my noise-canceling headphones. The noise . . . isn't exactly canceled. Sounds in New York City, I've learned, never stop. Trucks hiss all day and night, street produce vendors shout to each other every morning as they set up their stands, and during rush hour, people lay on their horns. It's not like Minnesota, but there's something exciting about being a part of the city that truly never sleeps.

Although, since Mom died, we've barely left the apartment.

Dad may be content spending twenty-four hours a day in this tiny apartment, but I want to see the city. A little bit.

"Welcome, I'm Mr. Parker, and I'm going to be your teacher for the next eight weeks."

All of our cameras are a little blurry and poorly lit, but his feed looks crisp. He's dressed casually, in a vintage tee with dark-rimmed glasses, and something about him just oozes coolness. I self-consciously run a hand through my disheveled blond hair.

Mr. Parker walks us through the syllabus, then takes the next hour to go in depth on the history of coding and some computer basics, some of which I know from my own research. Even so, I take diligent notes.

My eyes keep darting to my iPad, which has Riley's stream on it. In her all-white room, her jet-black hair pops out, and so do the pink cat-ear headphones she's wearing. She's laughing, seamlessly toggling back and forth between her console and her keyboard to chat with all the people viewing her stream.

Riley wants to do this for a living, and she's already well on her way. Even though she's only a year older than me, she already knows what she wants to do with her life. But then again, so do I . . . maybe. I guess that's what I'll find out this summer.

I snap back to the laptop as my teacher goes into more detail about the coding languages we'll be working with: HTML, JavaScript, and Python. Excitement thrums within me, thinking of all the different projects I'll be doing in this class. I've been begging to do this forever, and now's my chance.

For the quickest second, I picture my mom cheering me on, asking me dozens of questions about my assignments, and listening as I tell her all about the coding languages I learned about today while I help her cook dinner. A brief nostalgic moment, followed by a harsh ache in my chest.

I grit my teeth as I turn off Riley's stream—she's right. I can't afford *any* distractions.

Once today's lesson ends, I close Mom's old laptop with a sigh. This makes my brain hurt way more than regular school does. I started the day thinking I knew a lot about computers, but now I feel like I know nothing. This is going to be *a lot* of work.

But there's something captivating about it too. It's not exactly like Riley's passion for streaming, but I am interested in this, I think I'll be good at it, and maybe it'll be my thing someday.

My stomach grumbles, and I sigh.

I look into the kitchen from my spot on the couch, but a sad feeling takes over when I think through my lunch options. I like Hot Pockets as much as the next guy, but there's only so many I can eat before I lose my mind. And if you think about it, microwaved Hot Pockets and microwaved burritos aren't all that different: they're all frozen mush in some sort of bread wrapping.

I'm usually good about keeping my mind off my mom,

but *every single time* I eat a frozen meal, I wonder what recipe Mom would have made instead.

Even if I wanted to make one myself, I wouldn't know how. Some recipes she got from the old restaurant she worked at in downtown Minneapolis. Others she got from her family, and she could trace the origins all the way back to her ancestors in Hungary. I don't think a single person in the family wrote them down—they just taught their children how to make them.

Sure, I helped her sometimes, but not enough to know what I'm doing.

A light bulb flashes in my brain as I remember that one meal we'd make that never needed a recipe. We'd go downstairs to the produce street vendor, pick out a bunch of potatoes, onions, and whatever other vegetables that looked good, and make a . . . what was it called? A hash! That was always easy!

I take out my coding notebook and flip back a few pages, my heart falling when I read the title of each page:

Mom's Chicken Paprikash
Mom's Perfect Chocolate Chip Cookies
Mom's Palacsinta

Beneath each title are little scribbled notes from the corners of my brain, failed attempts at remembering each of these recipes Mom knew so well. The feeling of failure claws at me, but I turn a new page and label it "Mom's Breakfast Hash"—I know I can do this.

I scribble a makeshift recipe down in my notebook from memory. Then I dart to the fridge, excited about food for the first time in ages. I push past dozens of flavored seltzers to find an egg carton. There's only one egg left, and when I look at the expiration date, I sigh with relief when I see it's still good.

After running to my room, I sort through the change I keep in a jar by my bed. Four dollars and . . . twenty-eight cents. I'll start with the potatoes, onions, and hopefully I can afford a pepper too. That should be enough for a one-person hash, right?

I decide it's worth a try.

I grab the spare key and slip it in my jeans pocket, but I hesitate when I get to the door.

Yeah, I shouldn't do this. I know that. But . . . this feels important. I helped Mom make this meal every week. Sure, it's silly, but I know if I could just perfect one of her meals on my own, maybe a part of her will live on. Maybe I could make it for Dad someday, and we'd feel more like a functioning family again.

Maybe.

If Dad finds out, I'm toast. But I'll have plenty of time to cook, eat, and clean, and Mrs. Martinez isn't supposed to check on me until later this afternoon. My stomach grumbles again, and I decide it's worth the risk. I pull on my mask, grab a tote bag, turn the doorknob, and step out into the hall.

Mom's Breakfast Hash

INGREDIENTS

1 egg

~~2~~ some potatoes (it depends how big they are)

1 green bell pepper, ~~diced~~ chopped?

1 red bell pepper

1 onion (NOT the purple ones!)

~~garlic~~ (i don't know how to mince garlic, who am

I kidding??)

Salt

Pepper

Hot paprika (lots of it)

DIRECTIONS

Heat up the oven to ~~350 degrees~~ ~~400 degrees~~

375? (why does every recipe online have

different instructions?)

~~Cut~~ ~~chop~~ dice? the vegetables

(note to self: look up difference between dicing and chopping)

Put the vegetables in a pan and bake for 20(?) minutes, tossing halfway

Heat up a pan and cook the egg until it's over easy **I think I have to flip??

Put it all on a plate and eat?

CHEF'S TIP: It's okay if it takes a little longer than you were hoping. (Mom said this once when I was SO hungry and impatient!!!)

3

```
<!DOCTYPE HTML>
<HTML>
    <HEAD>
        ELI OVER EASY
    </HEAD>
    <BODY>
        <P>I MISS YOU</P>
    </BODY>
</HTML>
```

I listen for the sounds of footsteps above or below before I start down the stairs. Soft music echoes from upstairs, and I hear the super hauling in trash from the basement, but otherwise, the coast is clear. So I dart out the door and take quick steps down all three flights.

When I walk out the front door of our building, I'm hit with the staggering July heat. We only have two window AC units in the whole apartment, but they obviously do a good job, because this is unbelievable. I'm already sweating. This is nothing like Minnesota.

I wipe the sweat from my eyebrow and take a few long strides to blend in with all the passersby. I'm a little short for my age, which usually doesn't bother me, but in this sea of important businesspeople, struggling artists, and everyone in between, I feel like I stick out. The short Midwestern kid who can't stop staring into the sky at all the buildings.

It all says one thing: I don't belong.

But as I step onto the crosswalk, I get a glimpse of the Empire State Building, and it's so stunning that it makes me pause in the middle of the street. I've always known about this building, of course, but to be living in the same city, living within walking distance of it . . . It *is* kind of magical. The butterflies-in-my-stomach kind of magical.

If everything didn't smell like trash, and it wasn't so humid, the city could be perfect.

I cross the street to the familiar vegetable vendor who's set up camp over there. As always, the selection is overwhelming. Under the green tarp awning—which is shoddily propped up by milk crates—lies a stunning variety of fruits and veggies spilling out of cardboard boxes. After the Vietnamese woman who owns the stand finishes up with a customer, she gives me a warm smile, and I'm hit immediately with a wave of . . . something. Even though it's a bright, sunny day, it's like a shadow's just draped over me.

Maybe this was a mistake.

"Eli!" she shouts. "Where have you been?"

"I . . ." I trail off.

"Where's your mom been? She is my favorite customer!" She pulls her mask down to take a sip of her coffee, revealing the soft pink lipstick I've seen on her dozens of times. "She'll come back soon, right?"

I hesitate, caught up in nostalgia, and squeeze my fists so I don't tear up.

Do I tell her? How can I break the news to her?

"Yep," I say, avoiding eye contact. "Very soon."

I cringe with the lie, but I couldn't say the words: She won't be coming back. Ever.

"I'm making a hash, but I only have this much cash," I say. "It'll be enough for a big potato, an onion, and . . ."

She starts throwing vegetables in my bag. "Two potatoes," she says excitedly. "Green pepper, red pepper. What about asparagus?"

"But asparagus is five dollars!" I say, but she just waves her hand.

"For you, this is all four dollars."

"I . . . you really don't have to do this," I say. I don't know why tears are coming to my eyes, but I'd really like them to stop.

"No problem at all." She smiles politely. "My name's Ann. In case you forgot."

I try to slyly wipe a tear from my eye. I did forget, and now I feel bad about that too. But she was Mom's friend. This wasn't my world. Just like everything else, I'd tagged along, greedily waiting for whatever great meal was on the other end of the grocery trip.

"Thanks, Ann."

Out of the corner of my eye, I spot a familiar face. I turn and gasp. It's Mrs. Martinez, our neighbor, who appears to be walking home from the corner store with a boy around my age who I've never seen before.

The two of them laugh as the boy struggles to carry all of her groceries, and I can't help but let my gaze linger on his bright smile. His light brown skin and short brown hair glisten as he struggles to wipe sweat from his forehead with his upper arm. Without thinking about it, I mirror his action.

But then I snap out of it *fast*.

"I've got to go," I say quickly, panic rising to my chest. "Th-thank you."

"You got it," she says with a smile. "Tell your mom I say hi."

The sentence feels like a pinch, and I wince.

"I will!" I shout, my voice cracking with the lie.

I dash to the apartment building, ducking behind parked cars and keeping a low profile so Mrs. Martinez doesn't spot me. When a group of tourists pass, I hop up to the front door and let myself in quickly, hoping they've hidden me completely.

Once back inside the apartment, I wipe a few stray tears from my eyes. Tears of frustration from not being honest with Ann, the produce vendor Mom liked so much. Tears of panic from almost getting caught by Mrs. Martinez.

I close my eyes. Thinking back to the grief therapist I worked with for a little bit after Mom died, I sit with all my feelings for a second. Then I take a deep breath in from my nose and release it out from my mouth. The slightest bit of relief comes over me, then determination takes over, and I pack away all those negative feelings.

I fling off my mask and step confidently into the kitchen, pulling out everything I need to make this killer hash: a cutting board, a knife, a baking sheet, a frying pan. And, of course, all the veggies.

Cooking with Mom was never my favorite activity, to be honest. I wasn't even that good at helping her! Sometimes I hated cooking with her and *begged* for takeout. But now that I've had takeout every day since she died, I miss it all.

I miss the teamwork, the laughter, and . . . yes, I miss all those delicious smells.

I can do this. . .

I think.

After washing my hands, I start to peel the potatoes and prep all the veggies, taking extra care not to cut myself. This takes a long time compared to how quickly Mom could prep everything, but that's okay.

I carefully crack the egg and put it in a ramekin.

Mom always taught me to prep every ingredient, so that's what I do. She said working in a test kitchen was almost like having your own cooking show. You do all the prep work beforehand, so you have everything carefully measured out and ready to go when it comes time to cook.

Seeing all the veggies cut up like this, on the same tray, I feel a little bit of pride. So much that I take a pic and send it to Riley, with the text "Guess what I'm doing!!!"

That said, I still don't exactly know what I'm doing.

I put the baking sheet in the oven and then turn it on. I think Mom used to do it the other way around—she'd make me preheat the oven, but that can't make too much of a difference.

Next, I pour the egg into the pan and heat the stove. This is something I've never done before. Mom said she'd teach me how to make the perfect over-easy egg someday, but she never got around to it, or more likely, I never cared enough to learn. I've watched her do it enough times, though. It might not be perfect, but it'll be close.

Within seconds, I realize this is *nowhere close* to perfect. Something's gone wrong. The egg went from sitting, translucent, in a cold pan to cooking fast. TOO fast. But it's also not cooking at all in the middle. I turn down the heat, which was all the way up.

Maybe it's just time to flip, I think, so I fumble for a spatula and slide it under the egg. At least, that's what I'm trying to do, but the spatula goes through the egg and into the yolk. I realize with horror that this isn't a nonstick pan, and this egg is *definitely* sticking.

I know panicking won't help, so I scrunch up my face into a serious expression and try to troubleshoot the issue, like I would do with a broken line of computer code.

How can I save this?

Tears prick at my eyes, but I blame it on the onions and decide to flip the egg again. Little bits of it stick to the spatula as I go in for this second try, and the yolk starts running, turning rock hard as it hits the fire-hot pan.

This can't be saved, I finally realize. *I can't fix this.*

My tears are FLOWING now, and it doesn't have a thing to do with onions. The box I shut my emotions in just opened big-time, and there's no shutting it back down.

I'm such a failure, says the oh-so-helpful voice in my head.

I let the dark thoughts creep in. It's too heavy, everything is too hard, so I let my grief pull me to the floor. I sit and lean against the fridge, and I cry.

I may understand logic and computers, but I clearly don't get cooking at all.

My vision is blurred from the tears, but the smell of something bitter, almost . . . burnt, hits my nose.

"I didn't turn off the stove!" I shout to no one, jumping up to see the wreckage in the pan.

The bits of egg stuck to the pan are nearly black, but when I put on an oven mitt and jiggle the pan by its handle, some of the egg white still isn't cooked. The yolk is everywhere, and it smells like—

BEEP. BEEP. BEEP.

I yelp and step back from the pan. Looking up, I see the fire alarm going off. My brain is like the egg in the pan—a scrambled disaster. I run from the door to the window and back to the stove before I can let a thought come through.

Troubleshoot! I remind myself.

I quickly turn off the stove, then I grab the pan with a dishcloth and toss it into the sink. When I turn on the water, the pan releases a loud hiss, and a puff of smoke hits my face. *Crap.*

I dart to the window that leads to the fire escape. I open it and beg for the beeping to stop, but it doesn't.

"A cross breeze!" I yell and run to the door.

I can't let Mrs. Martinez see all of this, but she's bound to hear the alarm sooner or later, so I need to do whatever I can to make it stop. I prop open the door and feel a warm gust of air push pass me.

Good, I think. But the beeping doesn't stop, so I wrack my brain for more solutions.

Once I get myself back in troubleshooting mode, one comes to me. I grab our step stool and a throw pillow from the couch. Stepping up on the stool, I wave the pillow back and forth to blow some non-smoky wind toward the beeping menace.

As I keep the frenzied movement going, my dark thoughts block out reality. This never would have happened if Mom were here. If I had just let Mom teach me how to cook instead of resisting everything she said—

"Are you okay?" The voice snaps me out of my thoughts, and I look down to find the boy who was walking with Mrs. Martinez hesitating just outside my door.

The beeping finally stops, so I drop the pillow. It hits me in the face on the way down. I blush when the boy chuckles.

Tears prick my eyes again. *Not now*, I scold myself.

"Are you okay?" he repeats softly as this sweet, genuine concern comes over his face.

And for once, I'm honest: "No."

4

```
<!DOCTYPE HTML>
<HTML>
    <HEAD>
        ELI OVER EASY
    </HEAD>
    <BODY>
        <P>I MISS YOU</P>
    </BODY>
</HTML>
```

'm still standing on the step stool—drenched in sweat from a mix of the warm breeze cutting through the apartment, the heat from using the kitchen, and the sheer panic that still floods my veins—all in front of one of the cutest boys I've ever seen.

I've never been more humiliated. Except maybe for that time I fell off the stage during my middle school's spring musical . . . *and* the time Riley reenacted it to all of her followers on her most popular stream.

"My grandma sent me over here to find out what all the noise was about. Can I come in?" he finally asks, and I nod.

I step down from the stool, and even though it's only two steps, I still find a way to slip off one of them.

Great. Neat. More embarrassment.

"Something smells good," he says, and I laugh.

"You don't have to lie."

He shakes his head. "I mean, if you ignore the burnt smell, something else smells great. Peppers, maybe?"

"Crap! The hash!"

I grab the oven mitt and sprint to the oven.

"Can I help?" he asks.

"Um . . . could you shut the window? Between the heat wave and the oven, I'm dying here."

He closes the door behind him and makes his way to the window. He grunts as he pulls it down—it always gets a little stuck, but he's able to close it in one fluid motion. Meanwhile, I pull a tray of mostly burnt vegetables from the oven.

I turn it off and sigh.

"You're not from here, are you?"

I turn with a glare. "What do you mean?"

He laughs. "You just called it a heat wave, but it's eighty-five degrees. Which is pretty nice for July. Just wait for August."

"Oh," I say. I'd normally be embarrassed, but he doesn't seem judgmental, and this is probably the eighth most embarrassing thing to happen to me today, so I'm not too bothered. "I'm from Minnesota."

"Go Vikings," he says, then his face turns rosy. "Sorry, I have no idea why I said that. I hate football. Anyway, I'm from Yonkers."

I give him an empty stare.

"It's just outside of the city."

He takes a seat at the breakfast bar between the kitchen and the living room.

"I'm Eli," I say finally. "I should have led with that."

"You were busy." A smile lifts his voice. "I'm Mathias. Mat."

"Nice to meet you." I smile back. "Want some slightly burnt veggies?"

He nods, so I scoop them into two bowls. Even as I do, I notice how bad my knife skills are. Mom would have everything perfectly diced or chopped (I'm still not sure of the difference between those two), but the onions are too big, the potatoes are all uneven, and there are some seeds still attached to the bell pepper chunks.

"This is embarrassing," I say. I set his bowl and a fork in front of him before taking a bite. "And . . . I forgot to use any seasoning."

He laughs, but instead of making me sad or embarrassed, it makes me chuckle too.

"Way better than I could've done. Do you have hot sauce? Grandma says it covers up all sorts of sins."

We doctor up our bowls with salt, pepper, and hot sauce. I follow his lead to see how much to use. As I take a bite, it starts to taste better. Maybe even . . . okay?

"If you need help cooking, you could always ask her. She's pretty good. She can do about anything and never needs a recipe."

"It's okay. I think I'm done trying. Mom and I used to do this before she . . ."

"Yeah, I heard about that," he says quickly to fill the silence, then mumbles, "Grandma filled me in on all the details. I'm sorry."

"It's okay. I guess I thought I had more time to learn from her."

"My grandpa . . . he died from COVID, like your mom, but early on. Back when the hospital beds were all full in the city. Grandma got it, too, but when she had it, she barely had a cough. It all felt so"—he sighs—"random. I know it's not the same thing, but I guess I'm saying I know it's an awful way to lose someone you love."

"Mat," I start, but I don't know how to finish the sentence. His eyes meet mine as he offers a sad smile, and a wave of comfort comes over me knowing there's someone else who *gets* this. This . . . feeling of someone being snatched away from you in an instant.

I hear a knock at the door, and I can feel the color drain from my face. That is, until I hear the voice of Mat's grandmother.

I go to open the door, and Mrs. Martinez surveys the room suspiciously.

"Are you eating this boy's food?" she says sharply to Mat. "I thought I sent you over here to make sure nothing was on fire."

"No! I mean, yes, but—"

"I basically forced him to. Does this mess up your lunch? I'm sorry, I didn't realize."

She smiles and shakes her head. "I can barely keep this boy fed, he's growing so much. But, Eli, I don't remember your dad saying you were going to be cooking."

She looks at me, but my mind is blank. He didn't say that because, of course, I'm not allowed to be doing this. And everyone here can still smell the egg I destroyed.

"Just be careful," she finally says. "And Mathias, let's leave Eli alone."

He nods, and she disappears through the door.

"Well, I guess I'll be seeing you around. I'm living with Grandma this summer, so I guess that makes us neighbors now." He grins. "This was fun!"

His big smile makes me feel all fuzzy inside, and I can barely mumble a reply. "Yeah. It was nice."

I shut the door and blush as I try to figure out this new, warm feeling I get thinking about Mat. A goofy smile comes over my face, but as I turn to look at the kitchen, a groan escapes my lips.

Time to do dishes. A LOT of them.

5

```
<!DOCTYPE HTML>
<HTML>
    <HEAD>
        ELI OVER EASY
    </HEAD>
    <BODY>
        <P>I MISS YOU</P>
    </BODY>
</HTML>
```

After this week's breakfast hash flop, the only thing that motivates me to get out of bed every day is my coding class. Though we only have lectures three days a week, we have enough activities and instructional videos to watch that I've always got something to do.

All week, I sit through lectures from Mr. Parker and do all the optional practice activities. When I'm in this coding world, everything feels right. It even feels . . . safe, somehow. There's a logic there that I can depend on. Each new coding language I learn about, the more eager I am to stay in my lane as a coder—*not* a cook. Even if that means I have to eat some disappointing meals along the way.

Thankfully, Saturday morning breakfast is never a

disappointment. Dad and I sit in our usual two-top table in the corner of Hank's Bagels on Eighteenth Street, waiting for our order and taking in the ambience.

It's always a little chaotic, but the breakfast bagel rush at Hank's is next level. The restaurant is full of all kinds of people: families with strollers, NYU students who look a little too tired for eleven a.m., and people in various uniforms about to start their weekend workday.

In this corner, though, we get to observe and eat. As someone who is still a little unsure how I feel about New York City, there's a kind of safety in observing the city from the corner.

Then again, if I'm only observing the city from a corner, am I a part of the city at all?

An employee calls out our order, so Dad jumps up to grab our food. I pull my laptop out and set it up next to me, so I can get a head start on my weekend coding homework—although, since it's just the first week, most of the work is just watching introductory videos.

Dad hesitates before setting down his coffee and our bagels.

"It's always a little startling to see you carrying around Mom's computer," he says. "She took that thing with her everywhere."

"She used to work from Hank's sometimes, right?"

Dad shakes his head. "I think she preferred the coffee shop across the street. She was always into these fancy espresso drinks with oat milk—which is something I'm not even sure Hank's has heard of."

I laugh as I tear into my bagel sandwich: a toasted sesame-seed bagel with egg, cheese, salt, pepper, and ketchup. *Perfection.* After a week of frozen breakfast burritos—and one disastrous hash—I get ravenous as soon as I take my first bite.

"That was her favorite thing about the city," he says softly. "She couldn't work remotely much, but whenever they gave her a chance to write and polish her recipes from the coffee shop, she would stay there all day while you were at school."

I take another bite of my bagel, imagining Mom fitting in so smoothly in this city. Dad and I don't fit in the same way, that's for sure. But I wonder if we could, someday . . .

"I hear you got to meet Mrs. Martinez's grandson," Dad says, and a surge of panic almost makes me cough out my bite of food.

"Oh! She, um, told you?"

"I called her to check in on Monday, and she said you two got to meet."

I scan his face for any evidence that he knows anything's up—I wouldn't have wasted time cleaning up the kitchen so well if my cover was going to get blown like this! But he just digs into his everything bagel with lox spread.

"Right, Mathias stopped by and we talked for a bit." My defenses fall, and I let myself smile. "He seems fun. I hope we can hang out more."

"Sounds like he'll be around all summer. It'll be nice to have a friend next door."

I take another bite of my food, thankful that Mrs. Martinez didn't tell Dad about my cooking.

It took me *two hours* to do all the dishes and hide any evidence that I made that hash. I may have gotten a few things mixed up—I know where the baking sheets go, but what order did all the knives in the knife block go again?—but Dad is an even worse cook than I am, so he'll never know.

"Welp. Time to keep searching for new jobs," Dad says before pulling his computer out. He balances it on the small table, careful not to knock over his coffee or our food. "What all do you have to do today?"

"I have to watch three basics videos before Monday, and they're an hour each. I'm opening my first one now," I say. I tap into the school's program and open up the first link: *Basics of JavaScript*. It opens up a YouTube page with a video of a lecturer from the school. I put in my earphones and start the video before opening up my notes app.

I hit play on the video and get lost in my safe coding world once more.

As time goes on, Dad refills his coffee and brings me back an orange juice. I'm nearing the end of the first lesson, but looking at my notes, you'd think I'd barely started.

"Everything okay?" Dad asks with a concerned look on his face.

"It's hurting my brain." I shrug. "A lot of this is going over my head. I have a feeling this is going to get harder and harder every week."

"You'll catch on soon," he assures me. "You've always been more of a learn-by-doing kind of kid. How long do you have left? I think I have about one more cover letter left in me before I call it quits for the day."

"About ten minutes," I say.

Things . . . don't get any less confusing in the last ten minutes. I'm interested in it, but there are just so many words flying at me that I keep zoning out.

My gaze drifts around the screen, though, and I notice something I hadn't before: a little icon in the top right of the YouTube page with Mom's face in it. It's not too surprising that I'd be logged into Mom's account since this is her computer and all.

Idly, I click the profile picture and go into her You-Tube channel. I don't know what I'm looking for, exactly, but maybe it will show me some videos she watched before. I need a break from this dense class video anyway.

But before I can get to the section that shows viewed videos, I'm taken to a page with eight videos. Videos *she* uploaded. The channel's name comes into view: *Renee's Test Kitchen.*

Goose bumps cover my skin as I lean closer to the screen. In each thumbnail, she's smiling at the camera, holding up a plate of food. Some of the videos cover the classic Hungarian recipes that I was raised on, and others are recipes of her own creation.

Did Mom really make her own amateur cooking show?

I check the views on each of the posts, but quickly

realize the videos were listed as private. So no one could have watched them.

"Are the videos getting interesting?" Dad asks as he downs the last of his coffee.

I pull back, realizing I basically had my face pressed to the laptop screen in my surprise. I give a casual chuckle that ends up sounding a little like a hiccup, then shake my head. "Nope. I, uh, got distracted watching a different video."

"Maybe that's a sign we should head back home." He laughs.

I carefully close Mom's laptop and place it in my bag, as if jostling it even slightly would somehow make me lose access to those videos. I pull the backpack on and follow Dad out the door, my mind racing the whole time.

Did my mom really make her own cooking videos?

Could . . . could I learn to make some of our family recipes?

I don't know, but I can't wait to get home and find out.

On the way home, Dad suggests we stop by the street fair a couple blocks away from us. Of course the first time he suggests we do something fun and spontaneous in the city is also the first time I *need* to get back to the apartment . . . which I'm making clear by walking so quickly I'm basically out of breath.

"But what about our laptops in the sun?" I say, my mind scrambling for an excuse.

"Oh, they'll last awhile in our bags. It's not *that* hot out."

The sounds of the block party echo all around me, but I hesitate. I want to get home and watch these videos. But if I don't agree, who knows the next time Dad's going to want to do something like this. Lately, it's seemed like he hates the city: he hates commuting to his big office near Times Square, he hates doing anything touristy, and when he's not at work, he's almost always at the apartment.

A part of me wonders if Mom's death is why he hates the city this much. I mean, I think of her every time I walk past the produce stand. Anytime there's a street festival, or a parade, or something else bizarre, I think of her promises of a new adventure in such a wild, exciting city as New York.

I know Mom would drag us to this block party if she were here, and maybe that's why Dad's suggesting it. So I can't let this moment pass.

"Okay, let's go," I say with a strained smile. "But

we should make it quick, you know, so our computers are okay."

He laughs. "Deal."

My anxiety starts to melt away as we walk through the street party. On the left side of the street, a food vendor chats with a customer as the smell of sausages and onions fills the air. On the right side, a few kids push each other out of the way trying to get the attention of the Mister Softee truck.

"Want some ice cream?" Dad asks as we walk by. I do, of course, but the longer the line grows, the longer it'll take for me to see those videos of my mom.

"I'm okay," I say.

Dad eyes me suspiciously but lets it go. We continue down through the street fair past a DJ booth playing all sorts of songs, a lot of local shops handing out discount coupons, and (for some reason) even an inflatable bouncy castle. The kids inside are screaming with fun, and even though it makes me feel a little jealous, it's probably even hotter—and smellier—in there. So maybe it's good I'm too old for that kind of thing.

"Do you miss the trampoline we used to have?" Dad asks.

I realize I've stopped to watch all the other kids bouncing in the castle for too long. "Yeah, I miss a lot of things."

In the thumbnails of Mom's videos, I could clearly recognize our old kitchen. Our house back in Minnesota wasn't enormous, but compared to our apartment, it would seem huge. It had a yard just big enough for a trampoline, but we had to sell it along with our big furniture, even our car.

"Maybe we should just move back," he says. "Now."

I turn to him in surprise. "But I thought your job wasn't going to let you work from home anymore?"

"There are new jobs back home." He sighs. "You're right, though. They won't let me work remotely anymore, and I can't just quit out of the blue. What about you? If we could magically move back home now, would you like to do that?"

"I dunno," I say with a shrug. "I don't hate it here, but I miss Minnesota too."

"Once I find a new project management job back home, or a *real* remote one, you and I can make this decision as a family. You're getting older, and I know I haven't been treating you like it sometimes. I try not to be the helicopter dad, you know that, right?"

"I know, I know." I laugh as we meander back toward our street.

"I don't know what would be harder. Staying here, in the new home your mom built, or going back to our original home without her. What . . . what do *you* think?"

"I think . . ." I wipe a tear from my eye before spotting the Mister Softee truck again. "I think some ice cream sounds great."

6

```
<!DOCTYPE HTML>
<HTML>
    <HEAD>
        ELI OVER EASY
    </HEAD>
    <BODY>
        <P>I MISS YOU</P>
    </BODY>
</HTML>
```

It isn't until *seven at night* that I get a chance to hide away in my room with Mom's laptop. After Dad's stressful week at work, he wanted to get the most out of his Saturday with a Netflix marathon that led into yet another takeout pizza night. Thanks to plenty of pretend yawns on my part, I was finally able to sneak back into my room.

Sitting on the edge of my bed, I stare at the closed laptop.

Something feels . . . big about this moment. A discovery unlike any I've ever experienced before. Once, when I was watching one of Riley's video game streams, she stumbled upon this hidden door in a cave, and her chat was blowing up for *hours* as she explored the new area.

I slowly open the laptop and tap the space bar to bring it to life. As it does, a low battery warning flashes on the screen. As I scramble to get the cord plugged in, I think more about Riley's discovery. Part of why that was so special was because she could share it with other people. I can't talk to my dad about this, at least not yet, so . . .

I FaceTime Riley.

"Eli, what's up?" she says while casually stuffing noodles in her mouth.

I laugh. "Sorry, forgot about the time difference. Is Aunt Chloe mad I called during dinner?"

"No, Mom doesn't care." She shrugs. "I have a stream tonight, so I needed an excuse to duck out and slurp my lo mein while setting everything up. How's it going?"

"I found something," I say.

There's a pause on the other end as she starts the process of connecting all her streaming equipment.

"And that something is?" she says, kind of impatiently.

"A video of my mom."

Something clatters on her end before she quickly grabs the phone—I have her full attention now. "What kind of video?"

"It was this private video on her YouTube page. She was cooking. Kind of like she was pretending she had a show or something."

Riley gasps. "Show me! That's so cool! What was Aunt Renee cooking?"

Her excitement overwhelms me, and a weird part of me wonders if I should have kept this all to myself. It felt so private, this secret I had. But then I think of Dad and how uncomfortable and sad he seems whenever we talk about her.

I know I don't want to be like that, so I tell her:

"Honestly, I don't know. I'm just pulling up the video now. I was at the bagel shop when I found it, and I was trying to hide it from Dad."

"Hide it?" she says, leaning closer to the screen. "Do you think he didn't know?"

I shrug. "I don't know. Neither of them ever mentioned it. Maybe it was some secret that Mom was keeping. Anyway, you know how Dad doesn't like to talk about her much."

"That's not true," she says. "It might make him a little sad, but I bet he still wants to talk about her."

I shake my head. "You don't get it. He'll mention

her, then get real quiet, and then we'll spend the rest of the day in silence or bombarded with constant distractions—like today, we talked about Mom working at the coffee shop and we spent the rest of the day *and night* binging a Netflix show neither of us even wanted to watch!"

"Okay, I get it," she says. "I just don't know if you should keep this from him."

I hesitate. "I know you're right, but I guess . . . I want to keep this to myself for a little bit."

Riley doesn't have much to say to that, so during the silence, I open the video. It starts to autoplay, but I quickly stop it before Mom starts her introduction again. Seeing her face on the screen brings a tear to my eye, but I'm hopeful and excited too.

I flip the camera to show Riley the frozen picture of my mom.

"She looks so cheesy, I love it! She was always so much fun when she was cooking." Riley sighs, a little wistfully. "Ah, crap. I've got to start my stream now, but I demand updates. If you need me, give me a call and I'll throw up an ad break—promise me!"

"I will," I promise. "I'll tune in later if you're still on."

After the call, I've pretty much run out of excuses. So I hit play:

> *Hi, I'm Renee Adams and welcome to* Renee's Test Kitchen*! I always say that with a little bit of practice, and a whole lot of heart, anyone can be a chef.*

My heart aches, just for a moment, so I pause the video. Her voice is so familiar, yet so strange—she's pretending to be a famous TV chef, and I can't help but laugh when I replay the overly cheerful voice in my head.

I expected to feel something when I saw her talk. Of course I would—anytime I stumble upon an old photo or think too much about her I get caught in this web of grief. But I wasn't expecting to feel so nostalgic about other parts of the video: our old kitchen is in full view with its huge fridge with the ice maker, and its industrial-sized range with six burners. Everything feels huge and foreign, even though it's only been six months since I've set foot in that kitchen.

Riley's mom, Aunt Chloe, told me once that when it

comes to missing someone, the only way out is through. I can't hide from it, and I want to see more, so I take a deep breath and press play.

In future episodes, I'll show you some of my favorite recipes, but before we start with the complicated stuff, we need to work on basics. You can't make eggs Benedict without knowing how to separate an egg yolk for the hollandaise sauce, or even how to poach eggs.

My stomach grumbles—she did make the *best* eggs Benedict for weekend brunch. An English muffin, ham, poached eggs, and . . . that Holland sauce, or whatever she just said.

Eggs are, actually, the perfect place to start. In this episode, I'm going to teach you the basics of cooking eggs: fried, poached, boiled, scrambled, omeletted—okay, that's not a word, but you know what I mean. Let's start with a basic: the perfect fried egg over easy.

Inspired, I grab my notebook and flip to a page free of notes about coding. I write down all the steps to make the perfect fried egg. There's a lot of information, and I'm a little overwhelmed with even the basics.

I know I said I wouldn't do any more cooking, but maybe Mom's right: with a little bit of practice, and a lot of heart, I can be a chef too.

Eggs Over Easy

INGREDIENTS

~~1 egg....unless I mess it up.~~

*Many eggs

Salt

Pepper

Olive Oil (Do we even have that??)

DIRECTIONS

Crack an egg and put it into a ramekin or other

little cup (mom doesn't say why we don't put it

directly in the pan?) DON'T CRACK THE YOLK!!

Warm up a ~~skillet~~ nonstick pan over low heat

Put in a tablespoon of olive oil and shimmy the

pan around

Once hot pour in the egg (how will I know

when it's hot? Mom never says???)

Cook, flip, cook WATCH MOM DO IT FOR

TIMING

Sprinkle each side with salt and pepper, flip one last time

This is a lot of steps for one egg, wow

CHEF'S TIP: Take it low and slow. You're in no rush.

7

```
<!DOCTYPE HTML>
<HTML>
    <HEAD>
        ELI OVER EASY
    </HEAD>
    <BODY>
        <P>I MISS YOU</P>
    </BODY>
</HTML>
```

It's finally Monday. It's wild how long a weekend can feel when you're excited about the week to start—something I was definitely not used to during the school year. At coding boot camp, we have a packed week of tutorials, training exercises, and even a developer from a big tech company popping in for a guest lecture.

On top of all that? I have a new cooking experiment all planned out, and this time I *won't* fail.

After Dad leaves for work, I open up my laptop. On one tab, I pull up my coding classes, on the other, I pull up Mom's video. I'll have time to stop by the bodega downstairs and grab eggs in between my first two classes, then I will have all of lunch to experiment with them.

Mr. Parker makes us turn on our cameras for part of the class today as we share the things we've learned from the informational videos. It's the first time I've gotten to see the whole class since day one, and I notice for the first time that . . . everyone is way older than me. It's a diverse mix of people, but with the exception of myself, they're *all* adults.

I'm immediately intimidated, so I keep my mouth shut.

"Eli, you've been a little quiet," Mr. Parker says. "Sorry to put you on the spot, but what did you think about the videos? Anything interesting?"

"I . . . uh . . . I agree with what everyone else said." I blush as my mind draws a total blank.

He nods. "Okay, well, let's move on—"

"Oh!" I say, cutting him off. "Is it true that there are over seven hundred coding languages? I only thought there were a handful, so that blew my mind."

"It is true," he says with a smile. "And I'd guess there are even more than that. We'll only focus on some of the major ones in this boot camp, of course, but I'm glad you brought that up—I think it's important to keep in mind that coding is always evolving. So what you learn here might not directly apply to your future career, but you'll be able to take the skills you learn and keep growing."

As he continues speaking, I mute my microphone and breathe a long sigh of relief, glad I said something coherent.

Before I know it, the fifteen-minute break between our classes starts. I slip on my shoes, put on a mask, grab keys and my money, and slip out the door without a second thought.

"Morning!" the bodega owner says as I come in.

I give him a quick wave and wander over to the dairy section. There are a billion types of eggs here. Do I need free range? Farm fresh? Organic? Brown or white? Large or extra large? The timeline I'm on makes my brain short-circuit, so I just grab a carton at random. Eggs are eggs, right?

I get home just in time to start my next class. We're working on exercises this time, so I do my best to put my secret project out of my mind while I practice writing basic HTML code and start to learn exactly how computer logic works. I've practiced this a lot, so I fly through the exercises with my mind mostly focused on . . . eggs.

Eventually, class ends and I close my laptop with a sigh.

It's time.

I take my time preparing my ingredients, though there aren't many. I pull a ramekin out of the cupboard, grab an egg, and tap it softly on the counter. I look at the egg and see that I've barely broken it; only a little bit of the goo is coming out. So I tap again—harder this time.

And the egg shatters on the counter, my hand immediately smooshing into the gooey yolk.

Right, okay. Failure number one.

I dispose of the egg and wash my hands under warm water and disinfect the counter. Mom may not have taught me how to cook much, but she did teach me how to clean—touching raw eggs, raw meat, without washing your hands or cleaning the surface? Forget about it.

I try again with the Goldilocks approach. Not too light, not too hard, juuuuuust right. The egg cracks just enough for me to pry it apart over the ramekin. A little shard of eggshell gets in there, but the yolk is intact.

Success! Kinda.

I play back some of Mom's video, because I remember her talking about bits of eggshell.

And if you get some of the eggshell in there, don't worry! Here's an easy tip: Dip part of the shell into the liquid and scoop the shell piece out. The shell will attract itself, and you'll be able to get it much easier than if you tried to get it with your fingers. Just be careful not to crack the yolk!

I do as she says, and—*ta-dah!*—it works. And I don't crack the yolk. Step one down, eight hundred steps to go. All this for one egg?

I grab a pan to place on the stove, bring over the ramekin with the egg in it, and find the salt and pepper. I dig around the pantry, but olive oil is nowhere to be found. There's something called canola oil, and I wonder if I could use that.

But . . . I promised I wouldn't cut corners. If Mom uses olive oil, then I should too.

That said, I can't just go get olive oil from the store. I don't think I have enough money for that, and what if Dad saw the rest of the bottle in the pantry? I think through my options and eventually decide to ask Mrs. Martinez if she has some.

I leave the apartment and take the few steps to her door. I take a deep breath—if I'm confident and ask about it like it's the most normal thing in the world, she won't even know I'm not supposed to be cooking. Not like Dad exactly forbade it, but he probably wouldn't be so keen on me doing anything that involves fire, even if I sort of know what I'm doing from being in the kitchen with Mom.

I knock three times and wait, feeling my anxiety build with each passing second. Finally, the door opens, and a familiar face—one that doesn't belong to a seventy-year-old woman—stares back at me.

Mathias smiles, which makes me blush for some reason. He looks so put together, his bright floral shirt popping against his light brown skin, that I get immediately self-conscious about the graphic tee and mesh shorts I have on.

"Uh . . . hi, Mat!" I say, trying—and failing—to regain my confidence.

He just smiles. "Hey, Eli, what's up?"

I hesitate. "Well. I'm doing another cooking thing."

"Need me to start waving a pillow at the fire alarm?" he says with a laugh.

"I hope not," I say, blushing harder. "I'm just trying to learn how to fry an egg. Like, properly. But I don't have olive oil, so I was going to ask if you have any. I think I just need a tablespoon."

"Let me check," he says before closing the door in my face.

I wait awkwardly until he returns with a green glass bottle in his hands. "Here you go!"

"Thanks. I'll bring it right back," I assure him. "Unless . . . would you want to come over and . . . eat some eggs? I know that sounds weird; I just don't know how many tries it'll take until I get it perfect, and I don't want to waste food."

"I love eggs," he says quickly, then avoids eye contact. "I mean, I like eggs a normal amount. But sure, I can hang—Grandma's busy with a thousand-piece puzzle and I'd do anything to get out of helping her with it. Let me make sure it's okay."

Once we return to my apartment, he takes a seat at the breakfast bar overlooking the kitchen.

"What's the plan?" he asks.

"Eggs over easy." I wash my hands. "And every other type of egg I can perfect before I run out of them."

"I did not wake up today and think I'd be eating twelve eggs for lunch," he says with a laugh.

"I already broke one, so we're down to eleven. And I'll split them with you. Five and a half eggs sound doable?"

He shakes his head, but the smile on his face is beaming. "Let's do it."

8

```
<!DOCTYPE HTML>
<HTML>
    <HEAD>
        ELI OVER EASY
    </HEAD>
    <BODY>
        <P>I MISS YOU</P>
    </BODY>
</HTML>
```

feel like we're doing surgery or something," Mat says as I carefully lay out all my ingredients—oil, egg, salt, pepper—on the counter and place a small stainless steel skillet on the range.

"It really does." My heartbeat thrums through my body. "Okay. Oil?"

He hands me the filled tablespoon carefully and I dump it into the skillet, turning the heat on low.

"Egg," I say, in my best fake-doctor voice, while staring closely at the oil. "Apparently this will start to ripple when it's warm enough. Is it rippling?"

"No, I think . . . you're just breathing on it."

I pull back. Wait. Sigh. Shuffle my feet.

"Why does this take so long?" I ask.

He shrugs. "Just dump it in, it's probably hot enough."

I decide it probably is too, so I carefully plop the egg from the ramekin into the pan. And . . . nothing happens. No sizzle, no popping, and the egg white is as translucent as ever.

"Well . . . shoot," I say. "Okay, how do I save this?"

"Maybe just wait?" Mat suggests, but I shake my head.

"One time, Mom was cooking this pasta sauce and the oil was so hot it was splattering everywhere—she knew to pivot right away by turning off the heat and removing the pan from the burner before the kitchen got covered in red sauce." I turn the heat up and nod to Mat. "This is the opposite problem, so maybe I can just do the opposite: turn up the heat and get the egg cooking faster."

And it works. Well, kind of. Within a few seconds, the edges of the egg goo start to turn white. According to the video, this is when I should flip, but I know I can't flip an egg that's still 90 percent clear, so I hold steady.

I lean forward, watching the edges bubble, and Mat sidles up next to me to do the same.

"We . . . have no idea what we're doing, do we?" Mat

says. "Should I get my grandma? Maybe she could help us?"

I shake my head. "No, this is going to work. See? It's almost ready to flip!"

Mat sprinkles the egg with salt and pepper while I grab a spatula. I shimmy the tool under the lip of the egg and take a deep, cleansing breath. Without meaning to, a smile comes over my face: I'm cooking. And it doesn't even smell bad. It smells like . . . fried eggs!

"One smooth, fluid motion," I say, repeating the tip my mom gave in her video. "And . . . now!"

I push the spatula forward, but instead of sliding gracefully under the egg, it machetes *through* the egg, tearing the white up and clobbering the yolk. I stand frozen as the runny yolk turns hard immediately. Within seconds, the edges start turning brown.

"Oh no," Mat says before reaching over and flicking off the burner. I hand him the spatula, which he uses to poke the burnt egg.

"It got stuck to the pan," he says. "Again."

"Of course," I groan. "I still didn't use a nonstick pan! The *black* ones are nonstick. Why do they even make pans that stick?!"

Mat laughs.

"It's not funny," I snap, tears coming to my eyes. "My mom made this whole video about how to cook eggs, and she could always show me how to do things, but now she's not here and even these videos can't help me. I'm such a lost cause that I can't even cook an egg!"

"Hey," Mat says. I look to him, and I see his hand flick out toward me, then retract, a little awkwardly. Like he wants to console me, but he doesn't know how. And of course, how could he? We're not even friends.

I'm literally crying in front of strangers now. Nice.

"Eli, your mom is . . . was a really good cook, right?"

I nod.

"I don't think there's a good cook out there who's never messed up before. I mean, even my grandma messes up all the time—sometimes she'll put on some fried cheese, leave the room, and let the smoke detector tell her when it's done. Burnt to a crisp but she still makes it taste good, somehow."

I smile and look at the eggy disaster in the pan in front of me. "Sorry for snapping at you, before. It . . . it is kind of funny, actually. If Mom saw me now, she . . ."

I pause, but Mat jumps in. "What would she say?"

"She'd tell me to grab the right pan and try again."

He just smiles. "So let's do that."

▲ ▲ ▲

The second egg I make—in the correct pan—is better. Not perfect by any means, but better, and according to Mathias, it's edible.

"Maybe we should look up a different video," Mat says, and I sigh.

"No," I say. "I want *her* to teach me."

There's a silence that fills the room, and he offers me a soft smile that tells me he understands what I mean.

"Then we should just keep practicing. I want more eggs!"

I laugh. "I almost believe you mean that. Okay, I'll lower the heat this time and be a little more patient. And as soon as I flip a second time, I'll take it off. If you see that the white is runny, don't eat it, okay?"

"Got it," he says, offering a mock salute. "It's going to be perfect this time, trust me."

I do trust him.

We cook together, and as I prepare the ingredients, we talk more about his grandma and the type of cooking she does, and I learn more about his time in Manhattan. He's only been in town a few days, but they have plans to go see the whole city this summer.

"The Statue of Liberty, Central Park, and every

museum along the way," he says with a smile.

I flip the egg the first time, while Mat jumps in to salt and pepper the food.

"That sounds like so much fun," I say. "We went to Central Park once, but it was on the way to some dinner Mom had on the Upper West Side, so I didn't even get to walk around."

"Have you seen *any* of the sights since you've been here?"

"A little, here or there. Mom and Dad were just so busy with work, and I was trying to fit in at school— which I totally didn't, by the way—and the weekends we always just stayed in."

Mat shakes his head. "So all you get of Manhattan is this tiny apartment? No offense."

"No offense taken," I say. "I want to see more. But I don't know, Dad is a little nervous. If he knew I even went downstairs to the bodega to get these eggs he'd kill me."

I flip the egg one last time, Mat throws a dash of seasoning on it, and I quickly slip the spatula under the egg and transfer it to a plate.

It looks perfect. Soft, and a little jiggly. Cooked, but not too cooked.

"Let's make a deal," Mat says. "If this egg is cooked perfectly—I mean, runny yolk, the perfect over-easy egg—you'll come play tourist with me and Grandma this summer. It's how you can thank me for all my help."

"That's fair," I say. "I would have had to eat all eight of these eggs on my own if you weren't here."

I shudder at the thought.

"Moment of truth, then," Mat says, handing me the butter knife.

I decide then that no matter what happens, I do want to see the city with Mat. I want to explore and have adventures and not be trapped in this tiny apartment with nothing but my coding classes and sad thoughts to keep me company. Even if this isn't perfect, I'll go, if he'll have me.

I slip the butter knife through the egg and watch as the runny yellow yolk oozes onto the plate. It's the perfect over-easy egg. My mom has a million recipes and techniques that I have to master, but this was the first . . . and I did it.

I meet his gaze and pull him into a celebratory hug before I can talk myself out of it. He squeezes me back with a laugh.

"Guess you're going to see the city with me," he says.

"How about we start right now?"

"What?" I ask. "I can't leave, Dad would flip out if he knew."

"We won't even need to leave the building," he says with a smirk. "I'll grab the egg and our forks. You grab your keys. I'll lead the way."

Without another word, Mathias leads me out of my apartment. Though I'm confused, there's something about this that feels like an adventure.

When he turns left and starts to go up the stairs, I freeze.

"Where are you going?" I whisper-yell, in case anyone can hear us.

I blush as he flashes me a big smile. "The roof."

He leads me up the stairs to the fifth floor, and I feel immediate gratitude that our elevator-less apartment is not all the way up here. The stairway continues to a heavy metal door with a pretty clear message: Emergency Exit Only.

Despite our obvious lack of emergency, we approach the exit.

He lowers his voice to a whisper. "A couple years ago, I was visiting Grandma and Grandpa. I was bored to tears, but they said I couldn't leave the building, so I decided to explore. Grandma probably thought I'd just run off all my energy going up and down the stairs—which I did!—until I found this door propped open."

We step through the door, and the bright daylight blinds me as the heat smacks me in the face. I shield my eyes, begging them to adjust.

"I peeked out and saw the super was out here in a lawn chair, taking a lunch break," he continues. "I snuck back downstairs and went out on my own the next day, testing the door to make sure no alarm would sound. Of course, it didn't."

My eyes adjust just enough so I can make out my surroundings. For a second, I think it's going to be this dramatic, magnificent Manhattan landscape, but then I realize that you can't really see the skyline when you're only five stories up.

"Has the super ever caught you?" I ask.

We take slow steps around the flat concrete surface, and I feel the sun reflecting off it. I start sweating immediately. Mat wipes a sweaty cheek with his shoulder.

"Nah." He laughs. "He lives in a different building, so he only comes in on trash days. But look around! I love it here. It might not be touristy, and it might not be as impressive as One World Trade or any of those big buildings, but I still like it."

We're surrounded by taller buildings, but I can still peek through them to see other, larger buildings. In our neighborhood, it's all brick, but as I look farther south—or . . . what I think is south—bigger, metal buildings rise up and block my view.

"This is incredible," I say finally. "Look, you can even see the top of the Empire State Building from here, if you lean this way."

When I think of Dad's question about staying here or going back to Minnesota, I'm torn. With New York City, it's like there's always something new to discover. But new things are scary sometimes, and going back home sometimes feels like the best move.

We sit on the hot concrete and split the rest of the egg I cooked, and it's kind of like a picnic. There's something about this moment up here, with Mat, that feels special. Sure, I can't see the skyline, but who cares?

I don't need to see the skyline—because right now, I'm a part of it.

9

```
<!DOCTYPE HTML>
<HTML>
    <HEAD>
        ELI OVER EASY
    </HEAD>
    <BODY>
        <P>I MISS YOU</P>
    </BODY>
</HTML>
```

O ver the next two weeks, I eat a *lot* of eggs. Like, too many eggs for one human to consume. But my skills are improving, and that's what matters. And what's best is that Dad has no idea. Between the cash he leaves out for special lunches and my weekly allowance, I've got enough to buy cartons of eggs.

Today, though, I get to put all my skills to the test.

"Dad, I had a thought," I say. "Could . . . could we skip Hank's today?"

"Skip Hank's? But that's our oldest NYC tradition," he says with a chuckle. "Why, did you want to go somewhere else? Melody's Diner?"

"No, no, I was wondering if maybe we could cook breakfast," I say.

He pauses, and I try to read the thoughts in his blank stare. He's confused, obviously.

"I'm not a very good cook," he admits. "Not like your mom."

I shrug. "You don't need to be as good as Mom."

Because I will, I convince myself.

He stays silent, so I keep pushing. "We could go down to the bodega and grab some eggs, those frozen hash browns, and bacon or sausage or something. I can take care of the eggs if you can take care of the rest?"

"I don't know," he says, then sighs. "I know it's silly, but I've tried to stay out of that kitchen as much as I can since your mom passed. Kind of keep it as this greasy shrine. I'm not sure she'd appreciate me messing it all up."

I want to say that she can't appreciate or not appreciate anything—she's not here. But the thought is cold. The same feeling that's luring me into the kitchen is the one that's pushing him away. But I know if I could just get him in there, he'd get it.

"I feel like she'd appreciate her kitchen being used for more than breakfast burritos and chicken nuggets," I say, and Dad breaks into immediate laughter.

"You got me there." He sighs. "Oh, why not. You sure

you remember how to make eggs?"

"Yep, any style. I've watched Mom enough to know—fried, poached, scrambled, an omelette, you name it."

"You can do an omelette? I've even seen *Mom* mess that up."

I shrug, exuding way more confidence than I have. "Watch me."

Dad and I go to the bodega downstairs, and I instinctively go toward the eggs. I grab my medium brown eggs, a bag of shredded cheddar cheese, and some ham, and ask Dad to go get some potatoes. On the way back, he picks up some grapes and bananas, and looking in our basket, it looks like we have a full meal.

The gravity of what we're about to do is way more than what he knows. I'm not only about to try to cook something for my Dad from scratch—something I've never done before—but I'm going to try to prove Mom's theory right: that anyone can cook if they put enough work into it.

As we go up to the register, the bodega owner recognizes me and laughs.

"Egg boy!" he says, and I feel my cheeks blush. Thank god I have a mask on.

"What?" Dad asks.

The bodega owner looks at me, a little suspiciously. I shake my head, almost imperceptibly, and avoid eye contact. Though there's no way he understands what the heck I'm doing, he just laughs and apologizes.

"Sorry, I think I mistook your son for another one of my loyal customers. What brings you in today?"

"Well, we do need eggs!" my dad says, disarmed, then laughs along with him. "We're just cooking some breakfast together."

It's just a few words, but after three months of semi-decent frozen food, and takeout and delivery boxes scattered across the apartment, hearing those words fills me with determination.

That feeling carries me into our apartment and through the door. I send a quick text to Mat, inviting him over, but he says he's back home in Yonkers for the weekend and wishes me good luck. I set my iPad up and tune into Riley's stream, which has become a bit of a cooking habit of mine over the last couple weeks— eggs and video games. As I do this, Dad throws the hash browns in the preheated oven and gets to work dicing the ham to go inside the omelettes and putting together a makeshift fruit salad.

We both idly watch her stream while we prep.

"Wow, her setup just gets cooler every time I see it," Dad says. "Is that a neon-pink office chair?"

"Gamer chair," I say. "And yeah, it has cat ears too. It's awesome, and she's so good at it. She gains like fifty new subscribers every week."

I set the eggs out and set up bowls for the shredded cheese and diced ham. With one hand, I quickly crack four eggs and drop them into a mixing bowl. It's become second nature to me, having gone through dozens of eggs in the last week, and my stomach gets a little queasy thinking about eating *another* omelette.

But at least it's not a poached egg. Those were my least favorite, by far.

"Dang, Eli," Dad says. "You're quick."

I laugh, and for once, I tell the truth. "Mom taught me."

There's a silence, and I wonder if I've overstepped. We don't talk much about her anymore, even though she hangs over us. It's too hard for Dad, I know. But I like this. The smell of eggs and potatoes in the morning reminds me of her, and I like the reminders.

Dad . . . I'm not so sure what he wants. But he pulls me into a one-armed hug, so he must be enjoying this on some level. But before things get too sentimental, he switches the topic, pointing to Riley's stream.

"Ever think you want to do that?" Dad asks. "I'm not sure we have the funds for that kind of tricked-out setup."

"I'm not a big gamer," I say with a shrug. "But I love watching her play. She's so friendly, everyone just loves her. She's good at it too. One day she's going to be doing that for real, as an entire career, and who knows what I'll be doing."

"You know, I bet behind the scenes there's a lot of coding that goes on over there. Maybe you could work for that streaming company one day—you behind the scenes and Riley in front of the camera. Wouldn't that be fun?"

I chuckle, thinking that it's not a bad point. Every app, every website has a billion ones and zeroes behind it telling the program what to display, how to function. In my classes, we even got to hear from someone who works for a social media app. Her job seemed fast-paced and exciting, and I tried to picture myself in her shoes someday, far off in the future.

Back in the present, I toss a heavy sprinkle of salt and pepper into the bowl of eggs and start beating them by hand. With my first try making an omelette, I'd barely beaten the eggs, which quickly turned it into a scramble. The next time, I had the heat on too high and it turned brown before I could even fold in the ingredients. The third time, I don't even remember what went wrong, but it was so bad—and Mat was so full—that we had to trash it.

"Speaking of, how's your coding boot camp been?" Dad asks.

"It's so interesting," I say, even though I've only been half paying attention lately, focusing more on perfecting egg dishes. "I'm flying through the practice scenarios Mr. Parker's been giving us, so I'm getting antsy for something real. We're getting into practical projects soon, the one where we get to make a functioning site or app, and *that* will be fun."

He laughs. "As someone who was around at the dawn of the internet, I couldn't even tell you how it all works. It's kind of like magic."

"Cooking's like that too," I say.

I drop a pat of butter into the nonstick skillet and put it on low heat. Dad comes over and turns the heat up slightly, but I quickly slap his hand away and move it down. Believe me, I *know* what happens when you're impatient cooking any type of eggs.

"That was a play right out of Renee's book," Dad says, rubbing his hand dramatically. "She must have taught you a lot. I had no idea."

"We'll see if I can get this perfect," I say.

That'll be the real test.

Once the butter's melted, I pour in the beaten eggs and slowly rotate the pan. It's all silent, except for the random comment from Riley coming from my iPad—Dad's watching me closely, and I feel the anxiety prickling at my skin.

But when the warm, savory smell of butter and eggs hits my nose, my confidence grows. I've worked on this for two weeks. I know what I'm doing.

Grabbing a rubber spatula, I slowly slide the tip along the edge of the pan, shaking it from time to time to make sure the eggs are cooking evenly. Once they're firm enough, I pull the pan from the heat briefly to put in the ingredients—just cheese and ham—along the center of the eggs.

"Moment of truth," I say, returning the pan to the heat.

Dad leans closer as I flip a third of the omelette over to cover the new ingredients, then quickly roll it over onto the last third. The eggs are nearly perfectly cooked. Ideally, a perfect French omelette wouldn't have any color on it, but there's the lightest hint of brown in the center of the egg. But it's the closest I've ever gotten.

I transfer the omelette to a plate and tent it with aluminum foil so I can start on the second one, while dad flips the hash browns one last time. We assemble the rest of the breakfast *feast*, and for the first time in I don't know how long, we have a full home-cooked meal at the kitchen table.

Dad pours us a round of OJ and we dig in. I add a little more pepper, but Dad says it's perfect as is.

"You're telling me we could have been eating like this the whole time?" Dad asks, and I don't know if it's a joke or not. After a few bites, he sets down his fork and gives me an inquisitive look. "So . . . is that why they call you Egg Boy?"

My cheeks flush red and I stammer a response. "I . . . um, I think he was talking about someone else."

"Eli," Dad says with a sigh. "I'm so impressed with this, really I am. But I have a hunch you broke a lot of our rules to get to this point. I tried to ignore it—the lingering smell of eggs all week, the fact you took out the garbage every single day, the spare keys ending up in random places all over the apartment."

I deflate. "But I wanted . . . I wanted to cook more, like Mom."

"But you can't use the stove while I'm gone—it's *fire*. You could take down the whole apartment building. I know you think I'm being too cautious, but you're only thirteen, and Mom obviously showed you some tricks, but she didn't teach you everything. Things can still go wrong. I don't want to come home and catch you cooking en flambé and lighting your hair on fire. And don't get me started on you leaving the apartment— how many times does a kid have to go get eggs to get the nickname Egg Boy?"

I want to tell him about the videos, to tell him what I'm doing and why I'm doing it. But he'd lose it if he found out Mom didn't actually teach me anything while she was still alive. All I've really learned was from her videos.

So for now, I keep it to myself. I don't want to lie, but I know I'll lose this argument if I tell the whole truth.

"But I can't keep eating frozen food. And I don't want to eat takeout every night," I say, my voice wobbling. "I miss Mom's cooking, I miss *any* cooking. Please, let me do *something*."

He pauses to consider, but I can't help but think he doesn't get how much this means to me. Maybe if he saw how my coding notebook is full of half-formed recipes I'm trying to save, or if he watched Mom's videos with me, he would start to understand. Does this mean . . . I *have* to tell him?

He's going to be so angry.

I take a deep breath, ready to come clean about it all.

"No," he says in a deep, clear voice, catching me off guard. "No leaving the apartment to get ingredients, and no cooking—and that's final. We can cook brunch together on the weekends, but you can't do this while I'm gone, I can't risk that."

His words sting me as soon as they leave his mouth. He sees this as a risk? Sure, I might burn food every once in a while, but I can obviously learn—look at the perfect omelette I just made!

I set my fork down and chug my OJ, feeling trapped and misunderstood. But at least I can always escape to my room.

"I have coding homework to do," I say.

"Thanks for the omelette," Dad says, stern look fading from his face as I stand up. "It's perfect. This is . . . it's like old times."

10

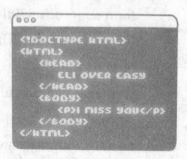

```
<!DOCTYPE HTML>
<HTML>
    <HEAD>
        ELI OVER EASY
    </HEAD>
    <BODY>
        <P>I MISS YOU</P>
    </BODY>
</HTML>
```

Though I briefly used to look forward to Mondays, this one feels like the ones I had at my new school in Manhattan. Transferring into a new school midyear was bad enough, but coming in as a country bumpkin from the Midwest brought a whole lot of additional anxiety.

From all the TV shows I've seen about transferring into a new school, I expected to be picked on for my glasses, or for not being a city kid like everyone else. What happened, though, was worse: I was ignored. No one wanted to get to know the new kid.

I had to introduce myself to the class that first week, and I explained where we came from, told them all about how my mom was a big-time executive at a test kitchen, where she prepped recipes for magazines and blogs, and how my dad worked in project management for a nonprofit wildlife organization. But in New York City, no one cares who your parents are, unless they're *famous* famous.

Though it was public school, my classmates' parents were VPs at Google, food truck owners, investment bankers, and everything in between. What really mattered was how interesting *you* were. And with my Minnesotan accent and my apparent lack of skills or interests, I . . . was not interesting.

If I were Riley, with my four thousand Twitch followers, maybe they'd care. But I was just a kid with a passing knowledge of coding. That is until I became the kid with the mom who just died.

When the teachers made my classmates send me "Sorry your mom died!" cards, I realized that even that didn't make me special. It was like everyone in the city lost someone to COVID somewhere along the last few years.

Middle school is hard enough. But is there anything worse than realizing that *nothing* about you is special?

After taking my first coding class of the day from

bed with my video off, I finally muster the courage to get up, shower, and make myself semi-presentable for the zero people I'll see today. The last few weeks, I had some purpose, but that all crashed this weekend.

So now I'm back to square one.

As soon as I finish getting dressed, the doorbell rings, so I shuffle over and peer out the peephole. All I see is Mat's very big eye, and I laugh before opening the door.

Once he comes in, he puts his palm on my shoulder and squeezes lightly, and I feel goose bumps flood my body. He's the first real friend I've made in the city, which is pretty special, but there's something else about him that I can't put my finger on that makes me feel *extra* special.

"What's the cooking adventure today?" Mat says. "Please tell me it's not more eggs."

I laugh. "No, no eggs. No *anything*. I . . . made an almost perfect omelette for my dad this weekend, but he pieced it all together and cracked down on me. So I guess I'm done with that."

"Oh, Eli, I'm sorry." He genuinely looks sad for me, and that makes me blush. "Grandma was talking with your dad this morning and he seemed extra worried about you, so that makes sense. Once they got off the phone, she said . . . well, never mind. It was kind of mean."

"What?" I say, scrunching up my face.

"She . . . said she wouldn't be surprised if your dad kept you on one of those leash-backpack things when you were a kid." He avoids eye contact. "Did he?"

Despite the slight, I laugh. "Ouch! He's just . . . overprotective. Mom was always the risk-taker of the two. She's the reason we're here, after all."

"Oh," he says, and we settle into the couch next to each other. "Do you think you'll move back, then? Would you *want* to move back?"

I'm opening my laptop, but the question makes me freeze. I keep trying to put off the answers to both of those questions.

"I miss Minnesota," I say. "But sometimes—like when we were on the roof, or how the bodega owner calls me Egg Boy, or when I peek out at night and see all of the people dressed up ready to go to fancy restaurants—I want to stay."

"And your dad?" he asks.

"He's job searching now. He does project management, which means he works with coders and gets websites built. He loved it when he worked from home, but something changed once his company decided to make everyone work in person. But if he's remote, he could do it from anywhere. I think he'll want to go back." I sigh. "What about you? I know you're in the city for the summer, but when are you moving back home?"

Now it's his turn to get awkward. "I'm not sure if I'm going back."

The tone in the room shifts, so I snap into Mom mode—setting down my laptop and going into the fridge. "Want a pop? Or some orange juice?"

"*Pop?*" He laughs. "Well, um . . . sure, whatever you're having."

I grab two Dr Peppers and bring them back. It was a weird instinct that just took over, but a comforting one. Whenever Mom sensed a mood shift or thought I was having trouble with something—like when I told her I couldn't make any new friends at school—she'd bolt to the kitchen to find me anything that would make me smile before we got into it.

"When Mom and Dad told me I was going to spend

the summer with my grandma, they made it sound like it was for her benefit—'She's getting older, she'll need your help, and you get to have a summer living in the city.'" He sighs. "I knew that wasn't the whole story—I mean, you know my grandma, she can carry like ten bags of groceries up to her third-floor walk-up without losing her breath once. I make it up two floors and want to pass out."

I laugh. "When Mom told me about this apartment she and Dad found, she kept saying it was a walk-up. But no one told me that a third-floor walk-up meant you literally had to walk *up* all those stairs. You see Manhattan in movies and everyone's got elevators and doormen and . . . yeah, this sure isn't one of those buildings."

"To say the least," he says with a smirk. "But when I went back this weekend to visit, things were weird. They tried to keep me out of my room, and when I snuck in there, I saw Dad had all his clothes in a suitcase in there. He had his razors and his soaps and everything in the spare bathroom."

"What do you think it means?" I ask.

He gives me a look, like *What do* you *think it means?*

"They're splitting up, I guess? All through Saturday,

I waited for them to drop the bomb, but they never did. Or maybe they felt like they couldn't. I don't know." A moment of silence passes, then he says softly, "I'm scared."

"I'm sorry, Mat." I rub a sweaty palm on my shorts and find my brain snapping back to Mom mode. "Do you want a snack?"

"No, no food," he says, placing his hand on my knee and smiling. "Just nice to have someone listen. I don't want to talk about it with Grandma, and my friends back home don't really get it."

The conversation drifts from there, and once his mood improves, he asks me more about the amazing feat that was my near-perfect omelettes, and I even show off the pictures I took of them with my phone.

"I know I told you I'd never eat another egg again," he says jokingly, "but I would *destroy* this. This looks way better than the ones you made for me; it's perfect."

I shrug. "My journey stops with eggs, I guess."

"Does it have to? You said your mom made other videos, right?" He pauses. "Do you want to watch another one?"

I shake my head. "It'll just make me sad. Not because I miss her—which obviously I do—but what's the point?"

"Could you try cooking *with* your dad?"

"Maybe. I liked doing it alone, though." I sigh. "Dad's been so different without Mom around. They were such a good balance—his cautiousness and her adventurousness, his mindfulness and her carefree attitude—but without her it's all unbalanced. This is the only time I feel like I can really connect with her, if that makes sense."

"That definitely makes sense," he says. "Well, I think you should watch another one, even if you don't end up cooking it. Just to get to know your mom better. And maybe you can practice with your dad later, once he gets used to the weekly brunches. Until then, is your cousin streaming?"

I flip to the Twitch app on our TV and scroll through. She's not streaming right now, it seems, so I put on one of her old videos. It's the one where she discovers the secret cave—it's already at thirty thousand views, and it's her most popular to date.

"You'd be good at this," he says.

"I don't really play video games," I say, rolling my eyes.

I know he's just being kind, but there's no need to lie here.

"Who said you have to stream video games?"

"What do you mean?" I ask.

He shrugs. "They stream all sorts of stuff on there that aren't video games, right? It was so fun hanging out as you walked me through every single step of making every single egg. I know your mom wanted her own show of her being perfect, or whatever, but I don't know—*Eli's Test Kitchen* has a ring to it, don't you think?"

11

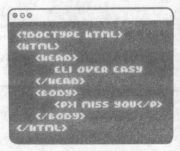

```
<!DOCTYPE HTML>
<HTML>
    <HEAD>
        ELI OVER EASY
    </HEAD>
    <BODY>
        <P>I MISS YOU</P>
    </BODY>
</HTML>
```

For the rest of the week, *Eli's Test Kitchen* lingers in my brain. But just a little bit. It's a good idea—people have entire careers on streaming platforms that just involve them chatting with their followers, doing silly crafts, bedazzling pillows, you name it. A live cooking channel would be fun, and new, and considering how half of my attempts result in absolute flops, I'd build a following on my cooking fails alone.

The problem is . . . Dad.

We're at Hank's Bagels again today, in our usual setup. My laptop faces the back corner, which is what gives me the courage to pull up another one of Mom's videos. I've only watched one so far, and in that video, she made it clear you have to nail the basics before you move on to more technical things.

It's a gradual learning process that's a lot like coding. Or, really, a lot like life itself. After Mom died, I wanted so badly to just wake up one morning and stop missing her. But the grief counselor my school set me up with helped me with coping strategies like remembering funny moments when things get too sad or staying close with family members like Riley.

I'm hit with a familiar wave of grief when I see Mom's face pop up on the screen. I know this pain will never fully go away, but lately—between coding and cooking—I've felt better. My eyes flick to my dad, who's cluelessly eating his bagel while job searching on the other end of the table. I keep the tears out of my eyes, and I breathe slowly as Mom's voice comes out of my earphones.

Hi, I'm Renee Adams and welcome to Renee's Test Kitchen*! With a little bit of practice, and a whole lot of heart, anyone can be a chef—even my husband, who is the most clueless cook out there.*

I smirk, wondering just when these videos were filmed.

We're going back to basics again today with my husband's favorite homemade pasta sauce. So this episode is dedicated to him. One day, James, I'll teach you how to make it yourself!

I start taking notes. Mom made the best pasta sauce, but it always took *forever*. Imagine smelling tomato sauce for six hours and not being able to even sneak a taste.

As she walks through the steps, I feel my cheeks getting warm with one part nostalgia, two parts stress. Eggs were hard, but they mainly consisted of honing one skill until it was perfect, or good enough, and moving on to the next. But this recipe has a lot of steps: crushing, dicing, simmering, stewing, stirring, all at the precisely right temperature, lest it all get burned or turned into watery soup.

No pressure.

"How much longer do you have left on that coding video?" Dad asks.

I pull out my earphones. "Um, a few more minutes."

"Great!" he says. "I'm wrapping up here, then I thought we would explore some."

My ears perk up, and I think of exploring the city:

the Empire State Building, Ellis Island, Rockefeller—

"There's a farmer's market down the street," he says. "We can see if they have any prepared food for dinner."

I sigh. Of course, his definition of exploring is *within three city blocks, no more, no less.*

But then his words finally register: a farmer's market!

I shut my laptop and again debate just how much to tell Dad.

"I want to make Mom's pasta sauce tonight," I say. "I think I can do it."

He pulls back. "But that takes forever. And you don't have a recipe."

"I found one online that's just like it," I say. It's not a lie. "We've watched her make it before, it can't be that hard. Maybe we could even invite Mat and his grandma over; you've never met him!"

I see the anxiety cross his face, but to his credit, he doesn't say no immediately. The thing is, Dad's always liked peace and quiet. He feels most comfortable at home under a weighted blanket, binging a series on Netflix. Mom always pulled him out of that comfort zone, but she's not here, so someone has to do it.

"Wasn't it your favorite meal?" I plead.

He raises an eyebrow. "It used to be, a long time

ago. But your mom made so much stuff for work, it was like I had a new favorite recipe every week. It's been years since she made that; how do you even remember me liking it?"

My cheeks flush. Truthfully, I didn't know that until I heard Mom say it on her video, but I just assumed it was a well-known fact.

"I remember the look on your face," I say quickly. It's not even a lie! The memory from when I was ten years old streaks back across my brain as I tell the story. "You tried to sneak a taste every time Mom went to stir it, and each time she'd tell you you'd burn yourself."

"And every time, I burned my tongue." He laughs. "But it was worth it!"

I keep eye contact with him, and I see his defenses break down. The peaks of his smile flatten; wrinkles form around his forehead. He releases a sigh that sucks the air out of the room.

"Why are you so into cooking lately?" he asks, his voice unusually soft. "You never wanted to help your mom in the kitchen. You used to be such a picky eater that we couldn't get you to eat anything that wasn't chicken nuggets for years. And, you might not remember this, but as a kid you used to hate this sauce because you saw the little green flecks of the basil in there."

I blush. "I just . . . think it's something I can be good at too."

He gives me a look, and I know what he's thinking: learning to be a good cook won't bring her back. Of course I know that. Of course I know that cooking won't fill the void she left.

"We should go," Dad finally says. "That sauce takes six hours, so if you want to eat today, we have to get going soon. Did you get an ingredient list?"

I pat my notebook. "Got it!"

While we walk to the farmer's market, I text Mat to ask him if he wants to come over for dinner. I invite his grandma too, though I make sure to stress to him that this pasta sauce might all be a disaster since I've never made it, and that there's a fifty-fifty chance we'll just be ordering in.

"We're in!" he texts back. "Grandma says she'll bring over an appetizer and some wine if your dad drinks it."

Dad and I grab all the ingredients we need from the farmer's market, except the tomatoes—those need to be canned whole, apparently—and a bottle of olive oil that we get from the bodega. Dad throws in a couple candy bars at the register, "to give us cooking energy," he says, and within minutes, we're on the way back to our apartment.

Dad unpacks the ingredients as I take out all the tools I need. I pull out Mom's old Dutch oven, which is this superheavy ceramic pot that you can use on the stove and in the oven, perfect for something like this. And I get out a cutting board, a few mixing bowls, a can opener, and a knife from the knife block.

When I turn back, Dad's barely unpacked at all. He's just looking at his phone.

"Whoa!" Dad exclaims. "That recruiter I was telling you about, the one who said he might have some leads for me, he just texted me to call him *now*. On a weekend? He must have something huge for me."

I pause. "Oh, that's great!"

We look at each other kind of awkwardly. I wanted his help, and he doesn't want me to do anything alone.

"Go call him. I can handle this."

"But that knife," Dad says.

"I'll be careful," I promise. "Mom showed me how to use it."

I can see he's torn, but eventually his excitement at the prospect of a new job wins out, and he says, "Okay,

I'll be back as soon as I can."

Right before he leaves, there's a knock at the door. Dad opens it to find Mathias in the hall.

"Hi, Mr. Adams!"

"This is Mat," I say quickly, "he's living with Mrs. Martinez this summer."

"So nice to finally meet you," Dad says. "And please, call me James."

Mat nods, then says, "Grandma wanted me to ask if you drink red wine. She was going to go get some if you do."

"I do," Dad says with a smile. "But she doesn't have to go out of her way to—"

"It's okay," Mat cuts him off. "I think she's looking for an excuse to have a glass of wine. Now that I'm around, she tries not to drink around me. But this is a special occasion, apparently."

Dad laughs. "Then red wine would be perfect."

"Can Mat stay and help?" I ask Dad. "If . . . that's okay with you, Mat."

"Oh yeah, of course," he says. "Anything to get out of puzzle duty."

"Sure, just both of you be careful. Please." Dad's phone starts ringing. "Yell for me or Mrs. Martinez if you need anything, okay? I've got to take this."

Once Dad leaves, I greet Mat with a big hug. It's not until I pull him into the hug that I realize that we might not be on the hugging level of friendship.

"You are . . . certainly not a New Yorker," he says.

"Is hugging friends a Midwestern thing?"

"A little." He chuckles. "I don't mind, though."

"Sorry, I'm just overwhelmed." I sigh. "I talked a big game to my dad about how I know how to do all this stuff, but I'm freaked. The only other time I've cut an onion was when I made that hash and, well, you know how that turned out."

He cringes. "Yeah, those onions were somehow burnt and raw at the same time."

I hand him my iPad. "Can you watch Mom's video—but put these headphones on—and talk me through the steps like she does? I'm not sure I can do it without her help, but Dad still doesn't know about the videos."

"Sure thing," Mat says with a smile.

He takes a seat at the bar looking into the kitchen, the spot he dubbed his egg-eating chair, and pulls up the video.

"She says to breathe," he says. "There are a lot of skills in this one, but they're all simple, and the best thing about it is that it all becomes one big sauce, so if your knife cuts aren't . . . good or whatever, you're fine, basically. Does that make you feel better?"

I shrug. "Not really. I'm still pretty sure I'm going to mess this up."

"With me and your Mom here, how could you?" Mat says with a smile.

And, despite my fears, I start to believe him.

The Perfect Pasta Sauce

INGREDIENTS

~~Fresh Tomatoes~~ whole tomatoes in the big can

Oil and butter, lots of it

Like a hundred cloves of garlic, ugh

1 onion (chop half and keep the other half
intact)

1 large carrot, peeled and cut into big pieces

Fresh Basil

*learn how to chefonade basil

*google how to spell chiffonade

Dried oregano, salt, pepper, and some other
seasonings

DIRECTIONS

After preheating oven to 300, dump all the
tomatoes in a big bowl. Use your hands to crush
them between your fingers until there are no big

pieces left in the bowl. WASH HANDS A LOT
AFTER OR I'LL TURN EVERYTHING RED

Heat oil and butter over medium heat in a large
dutch oven, sauté chopped garlic and onion, add
tomatoes and half the basil, then bring to a
simmer

Drop in the carrots and half an onion (only
for flavor! remember to take them out before
serving!)

Cover the dutch oven and place it in the oven
for six hours, stirring every 1-2 hours

Relax with a nice, cold Dr Pepper while Dad
boils the pasta

Top with the rest of the basil

CHEF'S TIP: Breathe. When things get too
stressful, just breathe. Remove the pan from the
heat and get your bearings. When you're ready,
put it back on and keep moving forward.

12

```
<!DOCTYPE HTML>
<HTML>
    <HEAD>
        ELI OVER EASY
    </HEAD>
    <BODY>
        <P>I MISS YOU</P>
    </BODY>
</HTML>
```

My hands are bright red, the kitchen is a disaster, and I'm on step *one*. Mom promises this is the easiest recipe in the world, but she didn't mention that this is also the messiest. See, squeezing tomatoes by hand in a bowl is nice and all, but no one tells you what to do when the tomato juice squirts out all over the counter, your shirt, and the floor.

"Whoa," Mat says. "That one almost hit the ceiling."

I grunt. "Why is this so messy?"

"Squeeze them lighter? Are you squeezing them outside of the bowl? Can you dunk your hands in and squeeze from there?"

"Ack!" I say. "I just got tomato in my eye."

Despite my obvious peril, Mat bursts into laughter. "See, this is why you need to stream your cooking mishaps. This is comedy gold. Can you turn to me for a second?"

I turn to him. My hands are stained red, my shirt is splattered with tomatoes, and I can't even open my left eye because of the juice dripping down my face. Mat, seeing me in this state, decides not to help. No, he decides to use my iPad to take a picture of the disaster.

"I'm sorry!" he says. "This scene was too good. Can I send this to your cousin?"

I sigh. "If I say yes, will you get me a towel so I can wipe this off?"

I hear the *shoop* sound of the outgoing message, after which Mat quickly comes over to help dry me off. He wipes the tomato sauce from my eye before handing me a towel. I take it to the sink and try to scrub the red away.

"You know, *now* is when I should've hugged you."

"I mean, if I were an inch closer, I'd have been caught up in the cross fire of those tomatoes. Here, I'll start cleaning it off the floor." He laughs. "Out of curiosity, is there any tomato sauce left in the pot?"

I roll my eyes. "You're being a little dramatic."

"Just a little," he says with a chuckle.

We continue cooking: chopping, measuring, and sautéing, and soon the smell of garlic and onion takes over the kitchen. My knife cuts are . . . not the best, but I learned how to cook things low and slow from my egg experience—*eggsperience*?—so nothing is burning. Yet.

With Mat's help, I pour the hand-crushed tomatoes into the pot and start stirring everything slowly, waiting for little bubbles to appear so I know it's hot enough to throw in the oven. I drop in a couple carrots, a handful of basil, and another quarter of an onion into the bubbling sauce, which boosts the flavor. I'll fish them out before serving.

"Is this a special recipe for you?" Mat asks.

I nod, just realizing tears are prickling at my eyes. "Mom said it was Dad's favorite, but smelling this . . . it smells like home. *Minnesota* home. Before we moved here and everything changed."

"Do . . . do you miss your mom a lot?" he asks.

I'm silent, but the answer is obvious. Of course I miss her.

"I try not to think about it," I say. "For the first few months, I could barely get out of bed. It didn't feel real. It still doesn't. Dad signed me up for a coding boot camp to keep me distracted all summer, one I'd been begging to get into for the last few years. I think both of us just realized that if we kept as busy as possible, we wouldn't have to think about it. We could just move forward. Push through."

Mat opens the oven as I slide the big bubbling pot onto the rack. I set a timer for sixty minutes. I grab us a couple Dr Peppers and we take seats on the couch as the ambient smell of tomatoes and garlic punches my emotions.

"Do you think this cooking stuff is holding me back? Or, like, making it worse somehow? I've been thinking about her more often, and I don't know if that's bad."

"I don't know," he says. "Grandma still talks about Gramps, and he died a few years ago. We still do all the traditions that he started. She still cooks his favorite foods. But I don't know why it would be bad to remember her like this. Don't you think she'd be happy that you're watching her videos, trying to learn from her?"

"Yeah." I smile. "She would. But I don't think Dad

would. Sometimes it's like he doesn't want us to remember her, but it depends on the day. Some days he's so alert and happy, other days the smallest reminder of her will set him off, and we'll be stuck in this long, awkward silence all day." I sigh. "I have to be careful with this cooking stuff. I don't want to be trapped in the past, and I can't make my dad upset."

"He might need the reminder too, even if he doesn't act like it sometimes."

Mat grabs my hand, just briefly, and gives it a squeeze. I feel my whole body blush, but before I can think too much about it, he yanks it away.

"Smells good!" Dad says, coming back into the room. "I'm sorry I couldn't help, but it smells like you two had it under control."

He peers into the kitchen. "Maybe I can help by . . . cleaning up some. It looks like someone got murdered in there!"

We laugh, and I shake my head. "No one warned me about the exploding tomatoes!"

Dad cleans as Mat and I finish our Dr Peppers. We watch one of Riley's old streams for a while, while I talk Dad through all the logistics of streaming. He doesn't quite get it, but he sits around and watches anyway, laughing along and commenting every few seconds how good the food smells.

He's got to be remembering Mom too right now. And he's smiling. This isn't everything, but it feels like a breakthrough moment.

13

```
<!DOCTYPE HTML>
<HTML>
    <HEAD>
        ELI OVER EASY
    </HEAD>
    <BODY>
        <P>I MISS YOU</P>
    </BODY>
</HTML>
```

Pasta night goes off without a hitch. The sauce needed a little more salt, and the onions looked like they got caught in a wood chipper, but for the most part, it was a good first attempt. Mrs. Martinez had nothing but compliments, and so did Dad, but as soon as I saw him tearing up while sopping his sauce with bread, I knew this was getting to be too much for him.

Thankfully, Mat and Mrs. Martinez didn't stay long. Since we said our goodbyes, we've been doing dishes. Dad washing, me drying, our awkward silence clashing with the campy "Italian Vintage Summer" playlist still playing through the Bluetooth speaker.

"I think I'm going to head to bed," Dad says after

we finish, even though it's only nine. "Thanks for the great food, buddy."

"Yeah, of course," I say, a little deflated to be left alone after something that was, I thought, this huge accomplishment. "Was . . . was anything wrong with it?"

"Hmm?" he asks distractedly, then covers his tracks. "Oh no, it was great. Perfect. Just as good as your mom makes. Made."

"You don't need to lie," I say, avoiding eye contact.

"Oh no, Eli—it was pretty darn close, I wouldn't lie to you about that." He hesitates. "Here, let's sit down for a sec."

We take seats on the couch, and Dad turns to me. There's something different in his approach this time, and I can barely sense it. But this feels like a grown-up conversation. Like getting *the talk* or something.

"Can I ask you why you're getting so into cooking?" he says. "I know that you and I would help Mom in the kitchen, but you were always so focused on your own passions: watching those old computer documentaries, coding that one website by hand. It's great that you found a new passion, I guess. I just want to make sure it is truly a passion, and that this isn't some cry for help that I'm ignoring."

I pause. This *is* a deep convo.

"I like cooking. I have no idea what I'm passionate about. I wish I was more like Riley, who has her whole life planned out, but I don't know what I want to do. All I know is this makes me happy, and so does coding. It's funny how similar they are too. It's all precision and logic and troubleshooting when things go wrong."

"But there's something different about cooking, isn't there?"

"I feel like the cooking is bringing me closer to Mom, in a way."

As I say it, I feel the littlest weight lift off my chest. It's the first time I've been honest with Dad about it, but it's also the first time I've been honest with myself about it too. I breathe a sigh of relief that gets cut short when I see Dad's watery eyes.

"Are you doing this because I keep leaving you alone?" Dad sniffles. "I don't want you to feel like you're losing me as a parent too, or that you have to pick up the slack for her, or anything like that. I'm still a little thrown that you *lied* to me when you were cooking all those eggs. You never used to do that."

"I didn't want to lie," I say.

"But I made it impossible for you to tell the truth?"

he says, not accusingly, just simply. I just shrug.

"Do you want to drop the coding classes? Maybe there are cooking classes I can send you to?"

I shake my head. "No, I want to do both. I just wish you'd let me cook on my own."

"I can't let you do that," he says, and I deflate. "But my original offer still stands. We can cook brunch on the weekends, and maybe even some easy recipes on some weeknights?"

I smile lightly. "Okay."

He makes his way to bed and I eye him along the way. Today's the most we've talked about Mom in a while, and though that's left me excited and refreshed, it seems to have had the opposite effect on him. He's drained, he's low.

But I keep thinking back to earlier today when I stirred the sauce, and he snuck a taste, just like he would when Mom cooked it. His eyes lit up, and he had a genuine smile on his face. I know that if I can just bring back Mom's cooking, it'll be like she gets to stay with us forever. And maybe that will help Dad start to heal.

And quietly, another thought enters my mind: maybe it'll help me too.

```
<!DOCTYPE HTML>
<HTML>
    <HEAD>
        ELI OVER EASY
    </HEAD>
    <BODY>
        <P>I MISS YOU</P>
    </BODY>
</HTML>
```

"Can I vent to you for a second?" Riley says, seconds after her perfectly lit face pops up on my iPad.

"Of course," I say. "Could we start with a hello?"

"Hello, Eli."

I smirk. "Hello, Riley. Now, what's up?"

"I had the most obnoxious troll in my stream this morning; he kept making fun of me no matter what I did." She sighs. "And you know what hurt worse? Only one or two of the people in the chat tried to shut him up. Everyone just like . . . watched, waiting to see how I'd respond."

My heart sinks. "Oh no, I'm so sorry. I wish I was there—I got caught up in this coding presentation and I had to have my camera on."

"Do you think you would have said anything?" she says after some reflection. "I'm being serious, it's not a trick question. I just . . . thought everyone would rush to defend me and they didn't. I'm just trying to understand why."

I think about it, hard. I put myself in the environment and imagine having Riley's stream on, watching the comments flood in. In one imagination, I snap at the guy and knock him down a peg. In the other, I hesitate.

I . . . know which one's more realistic.

"If I'm being honest, I probably would have waited to see what you said. You're so good at interacting with your fans and smacking down trolls, I would have been waiting to see you kick this guy's ass, then cheered you on with every emote I could."

She sighs. "I thought so. I think that's what everyone expected from me too. But I just wasn't feeling it today. I wasn't feeling strong and confident, and I just wanted to play my game and hang out with my friends . . . and now I feel betrayed."

I sigh. "If I catch it happening, ever, I'll make sure to speak up. I'm so sorry."

"Oh, Eli, I don't need you to be my knight in shining armor or anything." She rolls her eyes. "But the more followers I get, the more trolls come along. And god, they seem to *hate* me. It's getting exhausting."

I see the exhaustion in her eyes. It reminds me that even if she's living her dream, building her own streaming career and this huge following, she's still human—and not much older than me!—and I know I could never handle that kind of hate.

"You're really strong," I say. "I think that's why the chat likes you so much. It's like . . . I'm always comfortable when I'm on your streams because I feel safe there. I know you're going to make things cozy; you're going to make everyone feel special—I even get a rush of excitement when you say, 'Hey, cuz!' every time I enter. You always seem so in control, but maybe . . . maybe next time you could ask for help? Your followers love you, and if they knew you needed them, I know they'd back you up."

"It was so awkward. I just tried to play it off for a while, then I eventually banned him. I felt like a coward."

I wish I could give her a hug. "Hey, that's not being a coward. I'm just sorry you had to go through that."

She shakes her head. "It won't be the last. You know, I just realized I started streaming one year ago today?"

I remember it so vividly, but mainly because I was the only one who showed up for her first stream. This was before she got the gamer chair, the cat-ear headphones, the ring light. It was just plain black-haired Riley and the glow of her gaming computer.

"The Riley I knew a year ago would have quit altogether if she had a troll like that in her chat," I say. "But I bet you're already planning the next thing, aren't you?"

She smiles almost immediately. "I am! I'm playing a horror game next. FULL of zombies and blood and jump scares. It's going to be so funny, and I am going to make Aunt Chloe think I'm dying with all my screaming—you know how squeamish I am."

"Oh, I remember," I say, thinking back to our last sleepover before I moved to Manhattan. "Planning a scary movie night sounded like such a good idea. Until you started shrieking."

"Okay, venting is over. Thank you for making me feel better." She sighs, a hint of a smile in her face. "How's your coding going? Is it time to start working on your big project yet?"

"Oh god no—too early to be working on it. We're still drowning in tutorials and instructional videos. Mr.

119

Parker says everyone needs to settle on an idea soon, though, but I can't think of *anything*. It feels like every app has already been made, you know? I keep hoping something will inspire me, but I'm running out of time. Initial approvals for the app plan are supposed to happen soon, and then we get started in a few weeks!"

"I can't believe you're going to make a real, working app. I can't *wait* to see what you do. Maybe you can do something with cooking?"

I shrug. "Dad's really cracked down on that lately, so I probably shouldn't."

"So does that mean . . . no more cooking?"

I sigh. "I guess not. I couldn't pull off cooking eggs without Dad knowing; how would I pull off any of these bigger recipes?"

"He'll get better about it," she says confidently.

I'm not sure I believe her, though.

"Don't let this slip by, Eli." She turns her focus to the screen. "When you send me all of those photos—of the successes, the fails, and everything in between—I think about how awesome it is that you're doing all that. I know it'll be hard, but . . . you've got to try to keep it up, somehow."

An odd confidence bubbles up within me. "Okay. I

will . . . think about it, at least."

"Anyway, I've got to go fix my makeup before my next stream. Thanks for your advice—you're totally right. I put on this big front, because I have to, but my fans would tear these pathetic trolls up if I told them to." She gives me an evil grin. "I'm almost excited for the next one to come."

15

```
<!DOCTYPE HTML>
<HTML>
    <HEAD>
        ELI OVER EASY
    </HEAD>
    <BODY>
        <P>I MISS YOU</P>
    </BODY>
</HTML>
```

On Wednesdays, I don't have any coding classes. I start watching Mom's next lesson, all about the basics of cooking rice, and while Dad's at work, I've made a ton of notes on what to try for our next cooking night.

Around lunchtime, Dad gives me a call. As he does every single day. He still seems to hate his job, or at least hates being away from the apartment, but he only calls once a day now, which is a step up from how we started this journey last month.

"Hey, Eli!" Dad says, his tone unusually happy for a midweek workday. "I've got a surprise for you."

"Oh?" I say.

"Mrs. Martinez gave me a call—she said she's taking Mat to the Empire State Building today, and she wanted to know if you wanted to come along. It's a surprise for him too, since he's been having a bad day. What do you say?"

My chest fills with excitement. "Uh, obviously yes!"

Finally! I finally get to be a tourist in my own city. We've lived here for eight months, but I still feel like I know nothing that isn't within a three-block radius of me.

Right at one p.m., I hear a knocking at the door. I grab my keys, my wallet, and my phone and open the door to see Mat, who offers me a soft smile. The smile is a little off, and his eyes are a little puffy—almost like he's been crying. My chest aches as I pull him into another Midwestern hug.

This time, he hugs back.

"Ready for an adventure?" he asks, and I smile.

"I'm ready!"

Mrs. Martinez walks ahead of me and Mathias at a brisk pace, so brisk that I'm finding it hard to keep up! City walking is nothing like what I was used to in the suburbs of Minneapolis, where everyone takes their time. In New York City, everyone walks with purpose, and they will not hesitate to push you out of the way.

She keeps looking back, though, to adjust her stride and make sure she doesn't lose sight of us.

"How are you doing?" I ask Mat as we turn the corner onto Fifth Avenue. I can see the Empire State Building off in the distance, but it looks impossibly far from here. Sweat pools around my armpits, and I feel thankful I wore a dark blue shirt today, so the wet spots don't show.

Mat, though, seems unflappable. He's not winded, he's barely sweaty, and I envy his ability to navigate the streets like a real local. Even if he's not from here, his family is, which means he's definitely got a leg up.

"I'm doing okay," he finally answers. "More drama with my parents. It looks like they're splitting up. For real."

He charges forward, confidently, in front of me.

"Oh god, I'm sorry Mat."

He just shrugs. "I had a feeling it might happen."

"I mean, yeah," I start, "but—"

He cuts me off. "Why else would they be sleeping in separate rooms and sending their son off to live with a grandparent while they 'figure stuff out'? Of course that's what was happening."

We slow to a stop at a crosswalk, waiting for the

traffic to ease so we can cross the street. He sniffles but keeps his eyes straight ahead.

"I'm here if you want to talk about it," I say softly.

"There's nothing to talk about," he says quickly—not rudely, but it's short. He shakes his head. "They just dropped the bomb on me and immediately launched into this bickering about . . . custody, and me making choices."

His gaze finally meets mine, and I watch the tears form and sparkle in his eyes.

"I don't want to be pulled into this," he says. "I don't want this to happen at all."

I bump my shoulder into his, lightly, as we resume our walk. Just enough to remind him that I'm here. He looks at me with a half smirk.

"Growing up sucks," I say. "Like, it sounds so immature to say that, but it does, doesn't it? It's like . . ."

"You see everything changing around you, and you can't stop it."

I release a dry laugh. "Exactly that."

"Is cooking helping you?" he asks. "I know we're going through different things, so don't think I think this is the same thing or anything, but . . . it's really starting to hurt. All of this. I can't talk to my other

125

friends about it because they're all up in Yonkers. I can't talk to Grandma about it because she won't tell me anything."

"So you're stuck with me?" I say, half joking.

He smirks. "And you're stuck with me."

"One day, it'll feel smaller, won't it? All of this." And as I say it, I know that can't be true.

"Maybe," he says, and I can't help but think it's a lie.

"So let's make new memories today!" I say. "Fun ones that no one can take away from us, that have nothing to do with our families."

He smiles at me in return. "Deal."

The trek to the Empire State Building is as treacherous as I'd imagined—fighting to walk through groups of locals and tourists alike amid eighty-some-degree heat—but once we get there, I can't help but look up.

"It's making me dizzy," I say as I follow the length of the building, from the ornate art deco entrance to the light-up top. I've seen it from far away more times than I can count—it's like every street was built so that you'd have a good view of the building—but seeing it up close is bizarre and special.

And I can't wait to get inside!

Mrs. Martinez guides us to the entrance, and we're filed through the ticketed line to the elevators. We all pull on our masks as we're squeezed into an elevator.

"Keep breathing through your nose as the elevator goes up," Mrs. Martinez says as the doors close. "Your ears will pop easier that way."

Mat leans over and says, "She used to work as a secretary in one of those tall buildings near Times Square. I'd listen to her."

As we climb, I wonder if I've ever been this high up before. The elevator is gorgeous, even if I'm feeling a little cramped and claustrophobic smashed against so many other people, but what's waiting for me on the other side of the elevator doors is even better.

I step out and immediately see the view of the entire city through the plexiglass-and-wrought-iron fencing. We take our time to walk the perimeter, and Mrs. Martinez hands us a few quarters for the telescope machines.

"Which way is our apartment building?" I ask.

"Want to try to find it?" Mrs. Martinez replies, so Mat and I start mapping out the city.

"Well, One World Trade is south, so we're in that direction somewhere," I say.

"Broadway is that diagonal street, and that cuts right down near us."

I spot a telescope that's aimed straight down Fifth Avenue.

"Here, let's look through this one and see if we can find it!" I say.

We look and look, taking turns using the same machine, but from this high, all redbrick buildings kind of look the same, and to be honest, I have no idea what our roof looks like from this distance.

"Yeah, it's right there," Mat says. "Even if we don't see it exactly, that's basically where it's at. *Grandma*, you made us walk all that way?!"

She laughs. "Never stop walking! It keeps you young."

We roll our eyes and giggle.

I take photos of the skyline from every viewpoint, while Mat pulls me to different sections, showing me the Chrysler Building, Central Park, Times Square, and even the Statue of Liberty.

"See?" he says.

I turn to look behind me. "See what?"

"No." He laughs. "I meant *see*, I told you I would show you the whole city."

I blush so hard, my cheeks must be bright red. I take

one last look at the city, and among the hundreds of tourists . . . for once, I feel like this is my home.

We stroll through the gift shop without buying anything, and eventually make our way back outside into the scorching heat.

"A day like this calls for some ice cream," Mrs. Martinez says. "My treat."

I don't know how much of this is her being a nice grandma, which she certainly is, and how much of this is her trying to make up for everything Mat's going through, but he seems to appreciate it anyway.

We cross the street, and Mrs. Martinez flings her arm in the air to grab the attention of a taxi. Mat and I eye each other, and in some unspoken language, I get the impression that neither of us have ridden in a real cab before. I mean, why would you ever need to when Uber exists?

But I can't complain—hopping into a yellow taxi seems like a true New Yorker experience if there ever was one.

"Washington Square Park," she says to the driver, and we're off.

Mat leans over me to look out the window, and I

cherish his closeness, just a little bit. I've never bonded with anyone this quickly—it takes me forever to make new friends; that is, if I ever can make them—but somehow Mat has made his way into my life.

I shudder to think how many eggs this boy has eaten for me over the course of a few weeks. *That* is real friendship. And a part of me feels sad, because whenever we hang out, my mind will always say, just for one bright moment, *I can't wait to introduce him to Mom* before I remember, and everything falls apart.

But he is the first new friend I've made since Mom passed, and there's something hopeful about that. The only way out of grief is going through it, and going through it with someone like Mat makes it so much easier.

I don't know how long I'll be in Manhattan. I don't know how long Mat will be here either. But whatever happens, I know this is a summer I'll never forget. As he brushes my arm with his hand while pointing at the horse-drawn carriage we're passing, I feel a tingling sensation all over my body.

I hope he never forgets this either.

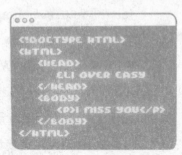

16

```
<!DOCTYPE HTML>
<HTML>
    <HEAD>
        ELI OVER EASY
    </HEAD>
    <BODY>
        <P>I MISS YOU</P>
    </BODY>
</HTML>
```

"So, what's your next cooking project?" Mat asks as we walk, ice cream in hand, back toward our apartment building after our mini tourist day in the city.

"Rice," I say. "Mom had this whole video on how to make rice, and I know a lot of it—when we'd make Chinese food together, I used to boil the rice while she'd make the rest of the dish. So I have that down, but there are still some techniques I need to work on. Like fried rice, rice and beans, other staples like that."

Mrs. Martinez stops in her tracks, so quickly I almost accidentally smoosh my ice cream cone into her.

"If you want to know how to make moro de habichuelas, you better let *me* show you," she says.

"He wants to use his mom's recipe," Mat says.

"His mom's recipe wasn't any good—she told me that in our very first conversation, back when you all moved in. As soon as she found out I'd been cooking it my whole life, she wanted me to show her." She pauses for a sad second. "We never got to do it, of course. You weren't here long before she got sick, really. Would you mind if I showed you?"

I fight back the tears. I always think of my mom as a perfect chef, but she never was—of course she wasn't! Her job was all about making mistakes and improving recipes. She'd jump at the chance to have someone teach her how to make something like this, and that reminds me that I shouldn't just be learning from her . . . I should be learning from everyone. Just like she would.

"Absolutely," I say. "When can we start?"

"We can stop by the bodega on the way up, and you and your dad can come over tonight. I'll make sure you get a feast—and you can be my helper the whole time. How does that sound?"

I feel the smile come across my face. "Let's do it!"

Dinner at Mrs. Martinez's apartment is so disorienting. In the short time since I've started this project,

I've always felt like I was leading the train, but this is totally different. I don't know where any pots and pans are, I don't know what some of these ingredients are, and I'm also dealing with the fact that this is an experience my mom always wanted to have.

Dad and Mathias hang out in the living room, sitting on unmatched sofas and lounge chairs and drinking tap water out of these antique glass goblets that are way older than Mrs. Martinez. Her décor is unique, split between centuries—the 1990s and the 1890s!—and I wonder how long she's been here.

The kitchen is older than ours too, and with how Mrs. Martinez swiftly takes out her pots, pans, cutting boards, and the ingredients she needs from a cupboard full of dozens of spice containers, this kitchen is her domain. Though it's a bit cramped, like ours—or, I'm guessing, any NYC kitchen—she maneuvers around me to set up a cutting board station.

In the back corner, between her coffeepot and microwave, sits a framed picture of her husband, beaming a bright smile. It's clear the kitchen is the heart of her home.

Before I know it, I'm on chopping duty. After the way I pulverized that onion for the red sauce I made,

I'm flooded with embarrassment when she hands me freshly washed cilantro and a knife and I freeze.

Seeing my panic, she slows down. This is her kitchen, so she can set the tone, and the timeline.

"Do you want me to show you how I chop things? I don't know if it's how your mom did it, and maybe the food blogs say it's totally wrong, but it's worked for me for quite a few years."

"I'd love that," I say, and take the knife in my hand.

She instructs me to hold the stalks of the cilantro and chop off the leafy parts. I throw the stems in the trash as she gathers the leaves into a tight pile.

"Okay, now you want to keep your hand like this," she says, and I'm gripping the knife like it's a magic wand. "You want to keep the tip on the cutting board, and you just rock the blade up and down, back and forth. Just like that, exactly. Now gather it into another pile and do it one more time—it doesn't have to be perfect."

She walks me through the same process with the bell pepper and onion. At the same time, she's working on the rest of the dinner—slicing the cheese, smashing plantains, and getting them both ready for frying. Everything already smells heavenly.

With her guidance, I sauté the vegetables and the herbs in a pot, then put in some chicken stock, red beans, and bring it all to a boil. Once I see it start to bubble, I add the rice. This is different from when we make white rice, I note, and instead of covering the pan, she has me keep it open, stirring occasionally.

While I tend the rice, she works her magic in the skillet, frying cheese and plantains and putting them on various platters. Once the smells of spices and fried foods hits my nose, a nostalgic feeling warms my heart. I may have taken all those times cooking with my mom for granted, but I won't let this experience go to waste: I grab my notebook and write about all the different food she's shown me today while Mat and Dad set the table.

By the time we sit down to eat, I'm ready to crash. It's been a long day, full of walking and exploring and cooking, but Mrs. Martinez still seems to have the energy to do it all again. I see what Mat meant, about how ridiculous it sounded that he needed to move in with her "to help her out."

As we sit down and serve ourselves family style, each smell makes my mouth water more. The semisweetness of the fried plantains, the richness of the fried cheese, and the masterful mix of peppers, onions, and spices in the rice.

I've never tasted food so flavorful—spices tingle on my tongue, mellowed out only by the starch of the fried plantains. We dig in and the home-cooked meal sits warmly in my stomach. This one wasn't Mom's recipe, but I can't help but think about how much she'd love this meal, and the experience of cooking alongside a seasoned pro like Mrs. Martinez.

I'm able to keep it together for the rest of the night, but as soon as I hit my bed, the tears start flowing. Cooking does weird things to you, and each time I cook something new, I feel closer to Mom . . . but also farther away from her.

Because I'm learning things with the help of other people—Mat, Mrs. Martinez, and even Dad. People that aren't her. And it's so unfair that she doesn't get to see this part of me. I'm going to become a hundred new versions of myself as I go on in life. She won't know Eli the coder, or Eli the cook, or Eli the high schooler.

And even though I've made so much progress . . . I can't get over how unfair that is. To her, to me, to Dad, to any of us.

<u>Mrs. Martinez's Rice and Beans</u>

INGREDIENTS

Onion (the purple kind . . . yuck)

Bell Pepper

Garlic (ugh, I need to practice mincing)

Cilantro

Tomato Sauce

Chicken Stock (Mrs. Martinez says I can use
veggie stock instead if I ever cook this for
Riley!)

Seasonings (adobo, oregano, pepper, and
others—I can't remember them all!)

Can't forget stars of the show:

Rice (and)

Beans

DIRECTIONS

Heat oil in Mom's big pot (Mrs. Martinez uses
a cast-iron one I can barely lift, but she says
a regular one would be okay too), add all the
veggies, stock, and seasonings, and cook until
the veggies start to get soft *IT TOOK US
ABOUT 4 MINUTES

Add beans and water and bring to a boil, then
add rice and reduce the heat

Simmer until the rice absorbs all the liquid,
stirring every once in a while once things start to
burn

CHEF'S TIP: It doesn't have to be perfect.

17

```
<!DOCTYPE HTML>
<HTML>
    <HEAD>
        ELI OVER EASY
    </HEAD>
    <BODY>
        <P>I MISS YOU</P>
    </BODY>
</HTML>
```

Though I only worked with a grief therapist for a couple months, I often find myself thinking about what she taught me. One lesson I always go back to is that recovery from anything—but especially grief—is *not* in a straight line.

It's highs and lows. Good days and bad.

Last week, at Mrs. Martinez's apartment, was one of the highest highs I've had since, but it led to the lowest low. It's like all the energy's been sapped from my body—I don't feel like cooking anymore, and I've been keeping my camera off in coding class, so I don't have to get out of bed. I keep waiting for something to happen. Some outside force to knock me out of this rut and put me back on track.

I know good days are coming; they *have* to be coming. But why aren't they here yet? Why *can't* recovery be in a straight line?

My phone vibrates, and I see Riley's FaceTiming me . . . again. I figure I can't keep ignoring her, so I flip to voice only.

"Eli?" she asks tentatively. "Eli, I did that new cat-eye makeup *just for you*, and you make this an audio call?"

"You did your makeup for your stream tonight," I say, my voice muffled by the covers. "You're playing that new cat game."

"Both things can be true at once." She hesitates. "What's going on? I feel like you've been ignoring me lately. You okay?"

Another thing I picked up from my therapist was to, you know, be honest about your feelings.

"Not really. Missing Mom, I guess."

"Oh, Eli," she says, and I hate being the one who makes her voice sound like that. "Talk with me, what's going on?"

I sit up, which feels like a bigger task than it should ever be, and tell her about everything. All my cooking adventures (and misadventures), and I explain my time with Mat and Mrs. Martinez late last week.

"Wait. Fried cheese is a *food*? Why did no one tell me this?"

"Riley, not the point."

She sighs. "Right. I'm sorry, babe. Let's talk through it, okay?"

"Okay. Um. Where do we start?"

"Tell me more about the videos your mom made. It's so cool that she's teaching you how to cook!"

I laugh. "Yeah, I guess so. It was one of the first things I thought of when she died. Isn't that weird? We were just on our fifth night of takeout for every meal, and I was like 'I wish I knew how to cook,' and that quickly tumbled into me regretting never learning from her."

"And you are now," she says. "That's *incredible*."

"But she should have been teaching me all along. I should have learned more from her, or I should have asked her about it, or something. I can't believe I never—"

"You can't believe you never thought to learn how to be a professional chef as a thirteen-year-old? Yeah, how could you?"

I laugh. "That's not what I mean."

"But it is, kind of? In no world were you going to be pretending to be a chef while you're also, like, learning

141

algebra. Who knows when your mom even learned. You can't give yourself a hard time for that." She pauses. "I mean, you *can* . . . you just shouldn't."

"I know you're right. Logically." I sigh. "There's just something so sweet about these videos. It feels like she's really talking to me, and helping me, and I had no idea she wanted to teach other people how to do it."

"Hmm," she says. "You could always post the videos publicly?"

"No one's going to see them," I say. "What if I post them, then they get like four views? Or worse, what if the trolls find these videos? They're pretty low quality."

"True, trolls are the worst," she says. "I had a few who wouldn't leave me alone in yesterday's stream, but I gave them a good verbal smackdown and they left. I hope they don't come back today."

Suddenly, I think of what Mat told me earlier: I could stream cooking videos.

"Riley, don't make fun of me, but can I run an idea by you?"

"I'm all ears," she says. "I'm pointing to the cat ears on my chair, which would have been funnier if we were on a FaceTime like we were supposed to be."

"If I did cooking streams, just like the gaming live

streams you do . . . do you think people would watch? I know it's mostly gamers on there, but there are all those cosplayers on there who do crafts, and all sorts of stuff."

There's a lengthy pause on the other end before she bursts into laughter. I deflate.

"Sorry, sorry, I was just picturing you streaming that tomato explosion disaster you were talking about." She laughs harder. "Yes, absolutely. Oh my god. Let's get you set up."

"Not yet," I say. "Let me talk to Dad about it. I've been lying to him enough, you know."

"Do you think he'll let you do it?" she asks.

"No idea," I say. "But it's worth a shot. Do you think I'll have problems with trolls, like you?"

She rolls her eyes. "First of all, you're not a girl trying to play video games for a living."

"Good point." I laugh.

"But there are always going to be some trolls out there. It's such a good idea, though. Just make sure you're prepared mentally—if you make a mistake and laugh at yourself, everyone will laugh with you, but if you make a mistake and get real embarrassed . . . and everyone else is laughing in the chat, it can really hurt. Take it from me."

I smile softly. "Thanks, Riley."

After our catch-up session is over, we end the call. I stare at the ceiling, and finally give in to my boredom. The only thing I can think of to get me out of this rut is watching another video.

I roll out of bed and open up my laptop, navigating quickly to Mom's cooking video page. I open the next video, and I'm thrilled at the prospect of learning a new technique. But I'm also a little nervous too. There are only a handful of videos left.

18

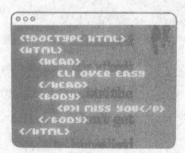

```
<!DOCTYPE HTML>
<HTML>
    <HEAD>
        ELI OVER EASY
    </HEAD>
    <BODY>
        <P>I MISS YOU</P>
    </BODY>
</HTML>
```

The next video starts playing. When my mom's face pops up on the screen, she looks a little tired . . . no, exhausted. She puts on a happy face for the camera, but I can see past that. She was always the kind of person who wore her emotions on her sleeve. Of course, I can only imagine what stress she was going through back when she recorded this video, but it reminds me that our life before New York City could be just as stressful as the one here.

Before she got her dream job at the test kitchen, she worked as a sous chef for a restaurant in downtown Minneapolis. She loved cooking for a living, but she hated the long, erratic hours. She hated being tired all the time. She hated the head chef.

145

She hated everything about her job—everything, that is, but the cooking.

My alarm goes off, which reminds me to stop what I'm doing and join my coding class. I quickly hop out of bed and bring my computer along. I grab a Dr Pepper, scramble some eggs quickly and pop them in the microwave (hey, as long as there's no fire, it's not *technically* against the rules), and set up my workspace on the coffee table in the living room.

"We're going to continue our JavaScript exercises today," Mr. Parker says. "While you're doing that, I'll pop in for our one-on-ones so we can discuss your end-of-term project."

The coding exercises start off relatively simple, but they scale up in difficulty rather quickly. We're nearing the end of our lessons on JavaScript, which is typical—as soon as I start to get a grasp on one coding language, they switch us to another. Of course, it's an accelerated intro-to-coding program, so maybe that's not so surprising after all.

I dive into my next project, thinking idly of the recipes that I want to make. Which ones would I even choose to stream? I know I should get Dad on board if I were to do something like that, but he worries so much about me cooking as it is, I don't want him to have to worry about trolls and harassment too. I see the kinds of comments Riley gets sometimes.

She may be unflappable, but I am very easily flapped.

A video request comes in from my professor through our instruction app, and I run a hand through my disheveled hair quickly, hoping I'm presentable enough for this.

"Eli, good to see you again," Mr. Parker says in a kind voice. "How are the exercises going?"

I shrug. "Not bad. I'm a little stuck on number eighteen, but I'll figure it out."

"Impressive!" He laughs. "Don't worry, you've got time. The last person was still on the fourth exercise; we all learn at different paces."

I nod.

"So if you don't mind taking a break from this, we should check in about your end-of-term project." He clears his throat. "You don't have to decide the specific format or coding language you'll be using until next month, but I would like to know what you're interested in creating. It can be as simple or ambitious as you want, and even if it doesn't work perfectly, I won't be too hard on you. I always say shoot for the stars when it comes to these things."

I think it over. "Honestly, I don't know what I want to do. It feels like everything's already been done."

"You don't have to invent anything; you just have to take a project and personalize it. Make it *you*. So, what do you like to do?"

"I've been into cooking lately," I say. "My, um, Mom's been helping me with some of her recipes and cooking techniques. But making a food blog seems so basic."

"Ooh, I see," he says. "Let's explore that more. I think there's a lot of opportunity for cooking and coding to combine, and it doesn't have to be a recipe blog. I'll go ahead and mark your topic down as 'instructional cooking,' and you should take some free time to brainstorm what you want to show. Have your mom help too!"

"Okay." I blush. "Um, yeah. I'll do that. Thanks, Mr. Parker."

"Anytime. If you want to send me some ideas before our next check-in two weeks from now, feel free. But remember, I'll need a fully formed plan for your final project then." He smiles. "But don't worry, I know you're going to do great!"

As we end the call, a faint feeling of dread comes over me. I wish I felt the same.

Once I finish up my work for the day, I return to my cooking notebook, flipping through the pages of scribbled notes to get to each recipe I've added myself. Mom's next video is a dish I've been wanting to make for a while, because it's something she made with her grandma as a kid. The sauce looks easy enough, and it all cooks in the cast-iron skillet, but there's only one problem: I've never cooked meat by myself before, and the dish is *chicken* paprikash.

So this will be my first time handling raw chicken, which is kind of gross. I need to be extra careful washing everything the meat touches, including my hands. And how do I make sure I cook it right so no one gets sick? This is a huge step up from everything I was doing before.

I play the video and write the recipe down in my journal, step by step and ingredient by ingredient. And that's when I realize that this dish isn't like her others.

Chicken Paprikash

INGREDIENTS

Boneless skinless chicken thighs, cut into cubes

Hungarian Sweet Paprika ("a healthy portion"???)

Flour

Sugar?

1 onion

2 cloves of garlic (I'm actually getting better at mincing garlic now!)

Tomatoes (it's some can, but she doesn't even say what kind????)

Chicken Broth ("just enough to make the sauce saucy")

Sour cream ("as much as feels right"? "the orange color will tell you"?????)

DIRECTIONS

Sear the chicken and remove

Cook the onion and garlic in the leftover

chicken grease (ew?)

Add "a healthy portion" of paprika and some

flour, and cook "until it feels right"

Pour in chicken broth and tomatoes, then cook

until the sauce is "real saucy" and "not loose"

then stir in the sour cream

Meanwhile, boil egg noodles in a big pot

Layer it like so: noodles, chicken, then sauce

CHEF'S TIP: Like Great-Granny says, "Trust

your heart." (Kind of nice but this means

nothing!!!)

19

```
<!DOCTYPE HTML>
<HTML>
    <HEAD>
        ELI OVER EASY
    </HEAD>
    <BODY>
        <P>I MISS YOU</P>
    </BODY>
</HTML>
```

he next day, I show up to Mat's apartment so his grandma can talk to me about cooking chicken.

"I'm not sure I can follow this recipe very well," Mat's grandma says, looking at the scribbled mess. "Is this all you have?"

"It's kind of a confusing recipe." I blush. Mom's videos are usually so step by step, so precise, but this one was all about cooking from the heart. "I mean, I took it from a video I saw. And that person, she, um, didn't explain much. For example, she just said, 'Make sure you cook the chicken enough' but I don't know what that means. How do you cook chicken and make sure no one gets sick?"

Mrs. Martinez sighs. "Can you show me the video?"

So far, I haven't shown these videos to anyone else but Mat. Not even Riley, and *definitely* not Dad. I trust Mrs. Martinez, of course, but the more people I tell about these videos, the higher the chance that this will get back to Dad.

But I have no choice. Either I have a good cook help me interpret this family recipe or I let it die forever. And even if Dad's okay leaving all that in the past, I'm not.

I get my computer.

When I return, I set it up on her coffee table. She and Mat flank me on the big fluffy couch as I pull up Mom's YouTube page.

"Okay," I say. "So, Mrs. Martinez."

"Is that Renee?" she asks as soon as the video thumbnail loads. She places a hand over her heart.

"Don't tell my dad," I say quickly. "Sorry, I know I shouldn't ask you to keep secrets or anything. But he's been so weird lately about me wanting to cook. You remember how that pasta sauce I made was one of her recipes? I found that on here. She has about five more, but she's using cooking terms that don't make sense. Here, let me show you."

Mom's face fills the screen as she rambles on about first learning this recipe with her grandmother. She's

153

oddly dodgy about measurements, using words like "a sprinkle," "a healthy handful," or "cook until it starts to smell really good."

I pause the video.

"This is what I'm talking about. All her other recipes were . . . recipes. I don't know what this is."

"This really is something." Mrs. Martinez laughs. "This is an *old* recipe. When you learn recipes that go back for generations, the details get a little fuzzy. Your mom learned this from your great-grandmother, and did you hear how she was able to list how each of her ancestors changed it?"

"Sure, but that part just confused me. So Great-Grandma used bone-in chicken thighs from the butcher, and Grandma went back and forth between boneless chicken breasts and beef tips—which sounds like an entirely different dish. And Mom used boneless chicken thighs, but what does all that matter?"

She puts a palm on my shoulder. "Because it's your family's history. A family recipe isn't truly yours until you've made your own changes."

"Okay," I say, though I'm still a little confused. "But what about the ingredients? What's the difference between a pinch, a sprinkling, and a good dash?"

"I don't know how to explain it, but maybe I can show you. I have chicken thighs and most of these ingredients. Do you still have Hungarian paprika at home?" When I nod, she turns to Mat. "While Eli gets the paprika, can you pick us up some chicken stock and sour cream from the bodega?"

With our assignments, we're off. Mrs. Martinez continues to play the video as I leave, and there's a strange comfort in hearing Mom's voice as she walks through the recipes.

That comfort shatters when I open the door and step into the hall just to come face-to-face with my dad. He turns to me in surprise, smiling softly.

"Dad!" I say, panic rising in my voice as I slam the door behind me. "Sorry I didn't tell you I was going over to Mrs. Martinez's."

As he opens the door, he laughs. "It's fine. She texted me to say you were making lunch together."

I follow him into our apartment.

"Are you feeling okay?" I ask.

"Better than okay," he says. "That recruiter helped me get a phone interview for this great project management position this afternoon, so I took a half day. It's fully remote, which means if I get it—fingers crossed—we could finally move back home."

My mind races, and I think of my time at the Empire State Building with Mat. Then I think of the bodega guy calling me Egg Boy, and Ann, the vendor across the street, who's always giving me discounted produce.

An odd thought comes to me for the first time: *This is home.*

I know we moved here for Mom's job, but there's something exciting about living in New York. I know the bodega workers by name now, I've made a new friend—two if you count his grandma. And I'm starting to pave my own life.

"Did you already start cooking?" he asks. "If not, I could get us some pizzas or something to celebrate. This is the first time a job just feels perfect for me."

"We're about to start," I say. "And I'm excited to learn some new techniques. Hey, what time is your interview? You could swing by after and eat lunch."

"Hmm, it depends how long my interview takes. Maybe you can bring me some back and give my compliments to Mrs. Martinez," he says with a smile. "What are you making?"

I smirk. "It's a surprise."

▲ ▲ ▲

I decide then that, regardless of how well this cooking experience goes, I need to come clean about Mom's videos. I hate keeping secrets from my dad. He's been loving my cooking so far, and I do feel like I'm getting better. And if I ever want to start streaming, we have to be on the same page.

As Dad prepares for his interview, I grab Mom's Hungarian paprika and return to Mat's apartment. His grandma's got the laptop on a folding table by the kitchen, and she's playing the video so loud I worry Dad will start to hear Mom's voice through the walls and think he's losing his mind.

"What do you serve this over?" Mrs. Martinez asks. "I haven't gotten to that part of the show."

"Mom used to serve it over those, um, twisty yellowish noodles?"

"Egg noodles?" she says. "Hmm . . . I don't have that, and Mat will be back from the store any second. I have a whole bunch of yellow rice I made, so let's serve it over that. It won't be the same."

I nod. "I bet that'll work just as well."

Mrs. Martinez turns on an old radio she keeps by

her kitchen, and music fills the apartment.

"Not sure how your mom did it, but I always think music helps you cook. It gets you into the rhythm of what you're making."

"I don't remember her playing any music, but this sounds good to me." I beam a smile at her.

Once Mat returns, we start to prepare the dish. Using the video as a guide, we prep the onions and garlic—under Mrs. Martinez's instruction, my knife cuts are getting so much better—and cut the chicken thighs into cubes and toss them in a little flour and paprika.

Mrs. Martinez lets me do the bulk of the work, coming in to add more seasoning every once in a while, and coaching me on the best time to stir. We sear the chicken in her cast-iron skillet and she tells me to wait until I smell the char before turning.

Before the chicken gets too dry, we mix the sour cream, stock, and a heavy portion of paprika. I pour it in and listen to it sizzle and pop.

"Is it done?" I ask.

"You've got to give it some time," she says. "The best thing I ever learned while cooking was patience. As a little girl, I always wanted to *stir stir stir* and get it over as quickly as I could."

"Were you a good cook as a kid?" Mat asks over my shoulder.

She laughs. "God, no. I'm still not a great cook—at least, I can't do all the fancy things those TV chefs do. But I know the basics. It looks like your mom would have made a nice TV chef; her smile is so big."

Tears prick at my eyes.

"I keep seeing Mom's videos, and I keep wondering what she wanted to say with all of these," I say. "With some of them, it's like she wants to land a Food Network cooking show; with others, she wants to get into the basics. And this one is mostly reminiscing while she barely gives a recipe."

"That's what cooking is, Eli. Real cooking. Maybe she wouldn't have had the best show, but I bet that's how she was taught to cook. I know so many recipes with ingredients just like this one—seasoning with your heart and not with a measuring cup. But my dad was really strict about teaching me the basics too."

"I wish she could have taught me for real," I say, a tear finally falling down my cheek. "I wish I would have cared more."

Mat comes around the table and gives me a hug, while his grandma takes the stirring spoon from my hand to finish up the dish.

I look into his eyes, and he just smiles.

"She's teaching you now, Eli."

20

```
<!DOCTYPE HTML>
<HTML>
    <HEAD>
        ELI OVER EASY
    </HEAD>
    <BODY>
        <P>I MISS YOU</P>
    </BODY>
</HTML>
```

I can still taste the paprika on my tongue. My body's filled with this warmth I didn't know I was missing. So maybe that's why, after I say my goodbyes to Mat and Mrs. Martinez, I smile to myself as I walk down the hall with a Tupperware of leftovers for Dad.

This dish wasn't a perfect re-creation by any means. Mom didn't sear the chicken as much before putting in the sauce, plus she usually served it over her own noodles, but it was close enough to bring back all those feelings.

Before opening the door, I take a deep breath. Once I tell Dad about Mom's videos, I can't un-tell him. But I know that now's the time.

When I open the door, the first thing I notice is the

smell of pizza. My heart drops a bit when I see the box on the counter, and as I walk past the kitchen and into the living room, I see Dad sitting on the couch staring idly at his laptop.

"Hey, Dad," I say. "How was the interview?"

He gives me an exhausted look, which answers it for me.

"It turns out the position wasn't quite as good as that recruiter thought. It would be a huge step down, financially." He sighs, then gestures to the leftovers in my hand. "Sorry, I wasn't sure when you were going to be back, so I just ordered a pizza."

"Oh, okay," I say. "Do you at least want to see what I made?"

He offers me a slight, encouraging smile, but I can feel the exhaustion behind his eyes. I cross the room to show him, but when I open the lid, he recoils, and I suddenly feel like I've done something wrong.

"Another of Mom's recipes?" he asks, irritation bleeding into his voice.

"Yeah," I say. "Chicken paprikash. It's a little different, because Mrs. Martinez likes to sear her chicken a little longer and we served it over rice instead of noodles. But it was incredible."

Dad nods. "Put it in the fridge. Maybe I'll eat some for dinner."

I cross to the fridge and find myself getting more annoyed with each step. I wasn't expecting a cooking award for it, but I was proud of this. I feel like I'm about to burst, so I take a deep breath and say the calmest thing I can manage.

"Why do you get like this every time we talk about Mom's cooking?" I ask.

When I turn back, his gaze is fixed on the wall behind me. He doesn't seem angry, or sad, or disappointed, just . . . neutral. Numb.

"Can you sit down?" he asks, so I do. "I was worried about this before, but now I'm pretty sure this is some sort of cry for help that I'm not answering. Or maybe I'm not even equipped to answer."

"It's just cooking," I say. "I'm having fun, and I actually feel like I'm getting closer to Mom, in a way."

He pauses for a few seconds, searching for the right words to say. "Maybe you should see that grief therapist again. Eli, I'm worried about you. For the first few weeks after your mom died, I started going through all the old birthday and Christmas cards we gave to each other over the years. I just read them over and over and over. I couldn't focus on anything else; I could barely get it together enough to order food for us every night."

"This is different," I say adamantly.

I think, a voice echoes in my head.

"Is it? How's your coding going? You haven't told me anything about those classes, and you begged us for years to send you to that online academy when you were old enough."

"Coding is fine," I say. "It's easy, I'm picking it up faster than half the class."

"So if I spoke to your teacher right now, he would say that you haven't missed any deadlines?" He pauses. "I'm seriously asking, not accusing here."

"Basically." I sigh. "We were supposed to pick a topic for our final project, but I haven't found one yet. But that's it."

Dad shrugs his shoulders. "It feels like you're stuck in this grief cycle, and I don't know how to get you out of it."

Without meaning to, I scoff. *Out loud*. Dad's eyes dart to me, demanding an explanation.

"I would rather be stuck remembering Mom than trying to run away from anything that reminds me of her, like you do." I clench my fists. "I saw how you looked at the food I cooked—you looked like you wanted to throw it right in the trash."

He gets up and starts pacing. "You're right, I want to move on with my life, *our* lives, and I don't think that's a bad thing. *And* I don't care whether this is a hobby or an obsession; if it's interfering with school, then you need to drop it."

I stand and grab my backpack with my laptop in it, then point toward my bedroom. "May I be excused?"

Before he can answer, I turn from him, barge into my room, and slam the door.

```
<!DOCTYPE HTML>
<HTML>
    <HEAD>
        ELI OVER EASY
    </HEAD>
    <BODY>
        <P>I MISS YOU</P>
    </BODY>
</HTML>
```

21

"**Y**ou stormed off and slammed the door on your DAD?" Riley's mouth makes an exaggerated O on the FaceTime call, but I just roll my eyes.

"Look, you don't think what I'm doing is bad, right?"

She shrugs. "I guess I can see both sides. But it's not like cooking has ruined your life, so that feels a little dramatic."

"I'm just tired of it," I say. "He will binge an entire Netflix show he doesn't care about while reading a book and texting his friends back in Minnesota just so he doesn't have one sad thought. Meanwhile, what I'm doing is enjoyable, and I think it's helping! Sure, it makes me sad sometimes, but it also makes me feel closer to her."

"Did you tell your dad all that?"

"Not exactly," I say. "My words get all jumbled when I'm in an argument."

"Then go back out there and talk to him about it," she suggests. "Unless you need to cool off first."

I shake my head. "I can barely think right now."

"Then go watch a few episodes of a mindless show, or listen to an audiobook, or something. Just take a couple hours off from the real world, and then go talk to your dad again when it's dinnertime." She nods. "I'll be streaming a new horror game today. Maybe seeing me get the crap scared out of me will improve your mood."

I laugh. "That sounds perfect. Thanks, Riley."

"Anytime," she says before disconnecting the call.

I open my laptop to find something to watch and jump back when Mom's face pops up on the screen. I guess I didn't close the browser before coming back. I want to close out, but something about her smile, her messy hair, and the dish of food in her hands makes me stop. Scrolling through her page, I see that I only have a few videos left. Maybe I can just watch one more video. Sure, maybe this is the wrong way to handle grief, I have no idea, but my mom put a lot of time into these fun videos, and right now, I want to watch them all.

The tone of *Renee's Test Kitchen* shifts a little, after

the scattered mess that was the chicken paprikash demo.

"Hello, and welcome! My producers have let me know that this is a terrible show," she says, her voice as cheery as ever. She winks at the camera, and I chuckle at the thought of her having producers for this one-woman YouTube show. I settle into my bed and listen to my mom tell a story I've never heard before.

I started this channel because I wanted to share some of my favorite recipes and share some of my favorite cooking tips. I had a passing knowledge of cooking growing up, but it wasn't until college that I really fell in love with it.

Every Friday, the girls on our floor would all chip in a few dollars, and I would use our dorm's communal kitchen to prepare a huge feast—bigger than you'd ever imagine coming out of that tiny kitchen. But I hated going to classes. I was an English major, but soon enough, the only thing I enjoyed about college—except the occasional party!—was cooking and trying new recipes for my friends.

I begged my parents to switch me into a cooking

school, even one at the local community college, but they wouldn't have it. They said that if I didn't have a four-year college degree, I'd never be able to make it in the world. I went to school the next day, sat down for my eight a.m. Literary Theory class, and when the teacher walked in, I got up and left.

I walked out of the classroom and into the administrative building and dropped out of college that very day. I drove from campus to downtown Minneapolis and walked into every restaurant to see if they were hiring for any back-of-house positions. That evening, I got my very first job offer. It was as a dishwasher for one of the best restaurants in town—or so I'd heard. I certainly never had enough money to go there as a nineteen-year-old!

Slowly, so very slowly, I started taking prep cook shifts. I'd learn everything I could from the cooks and chefs in the kitchen, and on slow days, they'd even let me practice some of their more finicky plating methods.

It took two and a half years, about as much time as I would have spent in college, until I landed a permanent job as a line cook.

I pause the video, wondering why I've *never* heard this story from Mom. I knew she never finished college, but she never told me she started out as a dishwasher and worked her way up in the kitchen. My gut twists—Dad must know about all this, right?

My favorite thing to do now, as an established sous chef—about fifteen years after I landed that first job—is to show new cooks the basics while also teaching them some of my favorite dishes. So, maybe this show makes no sense: day one, how to cook an egg; day four, a centuries-old Hungarian dish. But this is my show, and I guess that means I get to make the rules.

So, I'm bringing it all together. Today's lesson is both a recipe and a test-kitchen staple: the chocolate chip cookie.

She goes on to talk the imaginary viewers through her tips for the perfect chocolate chip cookie. She wasn't much of a baker, but she'd make these for us every once in a while. I don't have any sentimental memories of cookies, but I am fascinated by her process this time.

She makes one batch of what she calls "perfect" chocolate chip cookie dough, and then she makes a batch with some mistakes. While the perfect ones bake, she makes a grid explaining the difference between each dough. One has too much baking soda, one has too little. One has brown sugar, one has white. She explains that she's going to underbake a few and overbake a few, so we can see the difference.

You can't do something perfectly until you've messed it up every way possible first, trust me. And even then, you can make mistakes!

The video cuts to the fully baked cookies. She goes through each one and explains their pros and cons.

Underbaking them or overbaking them might ruin the cookie, but the other variants here might be right up your alley. Do you like a light and cakey cookie? Skip the baking soda and you'll have one like this. Do you want a thin, crunchy cookie? Use melted butter. Do you want it extra chewy? Chill the dough before baking, like this one.

This is . . . different from her other videos. Way more analytical. Scientific. It even feels a little bit like coding. I think of how I can apply this method to the times I've messed up cooking eggs or making sauces. As I think of it, my coding brain takes over and an app appears in my mind's eye, where anyone can make a dish and, if they run into an issue, tap the problem and get a solution.

I start sketching out the oversimplified code in my notebook:

```
IF{cookie is too crunchy}
THEN{chill the dough}
```

I shut the laptop and smile to myself. I think I've just figured out my coding project.

<u>Mom's "Perfect"</u> Chocolate Chip Cookie

INGREDIENTS

1 cup softened butter (not melted! Just not cold)

1 cup sugar

1 cup brown sugar, packed (note: look up what "packed" means???)

1 tsp vanilla extract

2 eggs (more eggs??? Pretty sure I am keeping the egg industry alive at this point)

3 cups flour (note: wear a white shirt, that flour is gonna go everywhere)

Baking soda, baking powder, and salt

2 cups chocolate chips

DIRECTIONS

Preheat oven to 375 degrees, spray a nonstick baking sheet with cooking spray

Mix the dry ingredients in a large bowl, then cream together the butter and sugar

NOTE: Mom uses a hand blender that I've never seen in my life?

Beat in vanilla then eggs one at a time

Mix in the dry ingredients SLOWLY (again, wear a white shirt)

Stir in chocolate chips, then scoop the dough out with a little ice cream scooper

Bake for 9 minutes exactly

Rest for a few minutes, then place cookies on a cooling rack

CHEF'S TIP: You can't do something perfectly until you've messed it up every way possible first.

22

```
<!DOCTYPE HTML>
<HTML>
    <HEAD>
        ELI OVER EASY
    </HEAD>
    <BODY>
        <P>I MISS YOU</P>
    </BODY>
</HTML>
```

"**S**o he just let you slam the door?" Mat asks.

We speak in hushed whispers as we trail Mrs. Martinez, who's leading us down Sixth Avenue. We want to be far enough back that the conversation doesn't get picked up by her ears—Mat swears she has the best hearing of any seventy-year-old on the planet—but we don't want to get left behind, and this lady is fast.

"Yeah, he was never big on, um, confrontation." I shrug. "When I did that to Mom, she would wait five minutes, gently knock on the door, then make me come out and talk about my feelings. I *hated* that. But I don't like this either. It's . . . awkward."

"That's not how my parents would handle it," Mat says between panted breaths. "Or maybe they would now. Lately, they're so tired, I bet they'd act the same way."

As we approach the next busy intersection, Mrs. Martinez steps out into the crosswalk as the traffic light turns red and waves us on behind her, putting her other hand out to stop traffic. Horns blare, but she doesn't seem to care.

We run to catch up and cross the street with her.

"I can't believe my parents made me think she needed help this summer," he says between panted breaths.

I laugh. "She's way tougher than me."

"You boys coming?" she asks, impatience creeping into her voice.

"We're trying, Grandma!" Mat whines.

She leads us into an area called Greenwich Village, and it starts to feel a little less like the New York I know and more like a peaceful, charming neighborhood. Of course, people are *everywhere*, but there's a strange quiet that takes over.

And best of all, it feels like half of the buildings have pride flags hanging from them.

We stop by a soft-serve cart to get some ice cream, and the three of us wander through the streets until we come across a small trianglular park. It's pretty unassuming, but she leads us over to a bench and sits down properly.

I sigh with relief as soon as my butt hits the bench.

"Oh, I didn't get us any napkins," Mrs. Martinez says. "You two stay right here. I'll run across the street to that restaurant and see if I can grab some."

Once she leaves, I turn to Mat and say, "Don't get me wrong, I love seeing new parts of the city, but why'd she choose this little park? We must have passed five others on our way here."

Mat laughs. "She . . . she's taken me here before. She'll talk about how great this area is, but she never asks any questions."

"What do you mean?" I ask, eating more of my ice cream.

"I think . . . she knows I'm gay. Which should be impossible since I haven't told anyone." He smiles. "She'll go a mile out of her way to hang out at the park outside of Stonewall, where we're just surrounded by pride flags, and just comment on how nice and accepting it is here."

"I think you technically just told me, for the record." I chuckle. "Same, I think."

"You think?"

I sigh. "Fine, I know. But I haven't exactly told anyone either."

"Cool," he says. "Our secret?"

"Sure," I say, giving him a smile.

We don't say much after that, but I don't know what else there is to say. I let someone in on a part of myself that I haven't shared with anyone—I thought it would be scary, but it was easy.

"I wish I'd told my mom, before . . ." I think out loud.

I feel my eyes prick with tears before Mat places a warm hand on my back. I turn to him and grin. "Sorry," I say.

"Don't be." He clears his throat. "I'm sorry you couldn't let her in on it, but I bet it wouldn't have changed anything."

"I haven't really thought about it much. I mean, I have, but not enough to, like, make a big announcement." I turn to him. "But I liked telling you."

"I'm glad you told me," he says. When he removes his palm from my back, I still feel it there, a phantom touch lingering, and it makes me blush.

Mrs. Martinez comes back in a huff.

"Would you believe none of these restaurants have paper napkins?" She sighs. "Not even little ones at the bar. Oh well. I guess we'll just be sticky."

"That's okay," Mat says.

"Thanks anyway," I add.

We finish our ice cream, and I watch a pride flag waving in the center of the park for a while.

"It's nice here, isn't it?" Mrs. Martinez says.

I look to Mat, who gives me a smirk.

"It is," I say.

The way back is every bit as frantic and sweaty as the way here. While Mrs. Martinez leads, I talk to Mat about my secret project.

"So basically, the app will have two uses. You can come in, choose the cookie style you want, and get a tailored recipe. So if you like crunchy, thin cookies, the recipe would be changed to have melted butter, with no refrigerator time. *Or!* Let's say you want to know what you're doing wrong with your cookies; you choose from a few preset issues. If you said they were too cakey, it would say to add more baking soda, or if you said they were burnt around the edges but raw in the middle, it would tell you to refrigerate the dough less and turn the heat down."

"You can really program an app to do all those

things?" he asks. "Like, would it be in the app store and everything?"

I laugh. "No, I don't think so. Not ... at first, at least. But I can get it working on a website for the project, and if people like it, who knows. And maybe I could do it with other foods too, like all of those egg tests."

"My stomach still churns a little bit when you say *egg*," he groans.

I cringe. "Sorry, sorry. I didn't want them to go to waste!"

"They definitely didn't," he says before burping.

I see our apartment building come into view.

"Mrs. Martinez," I say. "Can we stop by the bodega?"

She stops and glares at me. "Are you cooking something?"

"No," I say, then avoid eye contact. "Baking, actually. Chocolate chip cookies."

"I promised your dad I wouldn't let you cook anymore, and I wouldn't let you go to the store either." She sighs. "I'm sorry."

My gaze drops to the ground.

"I guess that's not too surprising," I say weakly.

"But I take lots of naps. And if Mat let you into the apartment one day, and you discovered that I had all the ingredients in my pantry, and some of those ingredients left my apartment . . . I guess I'd be none the wiser." She unlocks our building's front door, turns back, and gives me wink. "After all, I'm just a forgetful old lady."

23

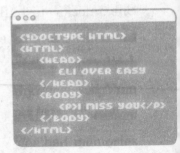

```
<!DOCTYPE HTML>
<HTML>
    <HEAD>
        ELI OVER EASY
    </HEAD>
    <BODY>
        <P>I MISS YOU</P>
    </BODY>
</HTML>
```

A week after our slammed-door argument, Dad and I have gone back to normal. Kind of. We never talked about it, but maybe things just resolve themselves after a while. Though, it doesn't feel resolved.

I get a weird feeling in my gut whenever we talk, and I'm not sure if I feel more guilty about the whole argument or the fact that I'm already scheming to break his rules.

But my cookie plan will only pull through if I can convince my teacher that it's a good idea. The exercises have gotten harder and harder, but I'm enjoying the challenge. And it really is like learning a different language. But I'm good at it!

I pull my scrambled eggs out of the microwave and

sprinkle a little cheese on them, then pour myself a glass of orange juice. I take small bites and sips as I set up Mom's computer for my one-on-one meeting with my professor.

"Eli, how are you doing?" Mr. Parker gives me a big smile. "Your exercises have been clean lately. Incredibly precise. The biggest mistake I see you make is forgetting to close your brackets."

I laugh. "I don't know why I keep doing that. I used this online coding tool for a while that closed the brackets for me, and now that we're coding things fully by hand, I can never remember that part."

"There are professional developers who still forget the end brackets, don't sweat it." He rubs his hands together. "All right, so have you finally picked a project for the end of term?"

"I have, I think." I take a deep breath. "So, my mom works—used to work at a test kitchen in the city. She, um, died a few months ago."

"Oh god, I'm sorry, Eli."

"No, it's fine, not the point, sorry." I blink hard to make sure no tears come. "But she made this whole video guide on how to make the perfect cookie. I was thinking of coding a visual guide as a web app, where you can troubleshoot the problems you have with your cookies."

He laughs, then clears his throat. "Sorry, I'm not laughing at you. These aren't usually the types of cookies we talk about in coding. Great idea so far, keep going."

"So, I have a few sketches of how it would look." I share my screen. "On the first screen, you'd choose whether you're here to get a custom recipe or to troubleshoot your cookie problems. The custom recipe would show you pictures—a picture of a thin, crispy cookie and a soft, doughy cookie—and maybe ask you to rate how crispy you want it on a scale of one to five. It would keep prompting you until it builds a custom recipe of *your* perfect chocolate chip cookie."

"I'm drooling already," he says. "I think you could make it a simple survey, but if you need help on how to export the final recipe, let me know. That might be a little advanced for our class. I'd also prioritize what tools you want in this app. You're the only one coding this, and you only have a couple weeks. If you have two features half-built, I can't grade either of them. Make sense?"

I nod, and he continues. "I say start with this recipe idea, and if you have time to develop the cookie troubleshooting tool, then great. Just keep me up to date."

"So my idea's approved?" I ask.

"Oh, absolutely." He smiles. "I love that you're doing something that's so personal to your family. But it's also a unique project. And it's making me want a cookie at ten in the morning."

I laugh. "Okay, great."

We end the call, and I open our test coding environment. I start playing around with some of the logic, plugging in some of the code I've learned and doing a *lot* of googling to fill in the blanks.

After a while, my phone buzzes, and I see Riley's face pop up on the screen.

"Hey, cuz," I say. "How was yesterday's stream? I didn't get to see it."

"Ugh, not great." She shakes her head. "This other popular streamer got all his followers to come into my chat and tell me how bad I was. He said it was a prank. He's just a jerk."

"Oh, whoa!" I say. "I can't believe that happened."

"He was just jealous," she explains. "My horror streams are going really well, mostly because I can't stop screaming at everything. He apparently streams scary stuff all the time but didn't like having a 'little girl' on his turf."

I blush, thinking about how we'd talked about me streaming my cooking fails. Even though she's only a year older than me, I've always looked up to Riley. If someone as unflappable as her couldn't handle the harassment, how could I?

"Don't you have moderators to help take care of that?"

"One of my streamer friends mods for me, but it was a mess." She smirks. "*Until* I remembered your advice. I knew my followers outnumbered all the weirdos in my chat, and I told everyone to spam the 'girliest' emojis they could find and drown out those misogynists. And they did—unicorns, flowers, sparkles. It was so hilarious but *so* epic."

"Heck yes!" I shout. "Now I want to go back and watch the recording."

"I'm still a little shaken by it all, but I'm glad I held my ground. Now I just need to get his hater butt banned from the platform. See how he likes *that!*" She shrugs. "Anyway, what's up with you? Anything newsworthy?"

"Well, I'm still not cooking. And I'm coding. And things with Dad are weird." I shrug. "I . . . think that covers it. But I do have a project I'm working on."

I go into all the details of my coding project, which gets me many oohs and aahs as I explain.

"I know video is your thing, but do you have any tips for taking photos? It's so dark here. I want to make all the different kinds of cookies, but I'm afraid all my photos will turn out all . . . dim."

She coaches me through what she calls "good social media lighting," and after a guided tour of all the nooks of our apartment, we locate the perfect area, with just the right amount of sunlight.

I spend the rest of the day coding and making a list of every cookie photo I need. Mat's agreed to let me come raid their pantry tomorrow morning. Thinking about lying to Dad again makes me a little queasy, but he hasn't left me much choice.

Maybe he'll understand, one day.

24

```
<!DOCTYPE HTML>
<HTML>
    <HEAD>
        ELI OVER EASY
    </HEAD>
    <BODY>
        <P>I MISS YOU</P>
    </BODY>
</HTML>
```

fter days of planning and late-night coding, it's
finally cookie time. My project doesn't work right
now—a couple buttons are right, but I have time to fix
the rest. I have about half of the cookie troubleshooting
feature coded, and I have the survey portion of the
custom recipe done. It goes against what my teacher
says, I know, but I got too excited. I know I can build
this; I just need to use my time well.

I also need to bake these cookies well.

From my spot on the couch, I hear a knock, so I cross
over to the door and let Mat in. He's carrying all the
other ingredients I need today in a little tote bag. He
gives me a smile, but something about it seems sad.

"Everything okay?" I ask, taking the butter from

him and placing it in the fridge.

"What?" he asks, then shakes his head. "Oh, yep. I'm excited to cook with you again. Well, bake."

"I'm excited too!"

I pull a spreadsheet up on my iPad and place it on the counter. It's got a checklist of every photo I need, and thus, every type of cookie I need to bake.

To start, I get all my measuring tools and ingredients out on the counter.

"What's your favorite kind of cookie?" I ask. "Crunchy, soft, cakey . . . describe it to me."

"Oh, huh," he says. "I guess I've never thought about it. But you know, I've always liked those thin, crispy ones they sell at the bodega downstairs. Do you know what I'm talking about?"

"Ooh, wrong answer." I shake my head. "I'm more of a soft-cookie kind of guy. Guess this friendship was doomed from the start."

He laughs, but there's still something a little off about him today. He's not his bubbly self, he's got this presence hanging over him. It reminds me of how I felt, and still feel sometimes, after Mom passed. Kind of like you're walking through a haze so thick you can barely breathe, but you have to keep smiling.

Of course, I'm probably just overanalyzing it. Cookies might not fix everything, but they can help any bad mood. So I decide to start with a batch of thin, crispy cookies. Just for him.

We follow Mom's recipe, and a focus takes over the kitchen. This isn't like the egg experience—that was totally one-sided. This time, I'm cooking with someone, just like when I cooked with Mrs. Martinez.

I hand him a whisk and he starts stirring the dry ingredients as I sift flour into the bowl. He watches as I cream the butter and sugar together, and once the dough is mixed, we make perfectly even balls of dough and plop them onto the baking sheet. Our hands are all sticky, flour is everywhere, but a strange calm comes over me when the smell of vanilla fills the air.

"I like baking with you," I say. "And I like cooking with your grandma. I always thought cooking was all a solitary thing, unless you worked in a kitchen of course, but doing this with someone else is so fun."

A genuine smile comes across his face. "Aw, I like baking with you too."

We only have two baking sheets, so it's basically an assembly line from one batch to the next. After the thin and crispy ones come out of the oven, I place them on a cooling rack and swap in a batch of Mom's "perfect" chocolate chip cookies. I place a few leftovers in the fridge so when I bake those, they'll be a little more squishy. (How *I* like them.)

As I go to start a new batch . . . this is where things get a little complicated. Thankfully I have my spreadsheet to help. I make smaller mixes—some with no baking soda, some with more flour, some with brown sugar, white sugar.

I also make a few intentional mistakes. Whisking too much, not whisking enough, adding too much baking soda. From the original mix, I also plan to intentionally burn a few and pull a few out too early.

"This is . . . complicated," Mat says, and I laugh.

"Do you want to take a break?" I ask.

After considering it for a while, he nods. Once I put the next batch in, we wash our hands, and I grab one of Mom's "perfect" cookies and one of Mat's crispy cookies and take them into the living room. We devour them so quickly, I barely have time to register how good they taste, but a sweet buttery flavor lingers in my mouth that makes me want to go grab another right away.

It takes a few hours, but once all the baking's done, Mat takes care of the many dishes while I set up a makeshift photography studio. (Really, it's just a tablecloth on a side table with the perfect amount of sunlight coming in from our front window.)

We put the dishes away together, and I take one last look at the oven and counters for any sign we'd been cooking.

"Well," I say. "The smell of cookies is inescapable. There are also four dozen cookies sitting on the counter. But other than that, you'd never know we were baking today."

Mat turns to me and laughs, then brushes a thumb down the tip of my nose.

"You've got flour all over too."

"I'll shower and change clothes before Dad gets back," I say with a smile.

Methodically, we photograph and catalog each of the cookie variants. I save each photo to a folder on my phone, so I can upload them all to a cloud drive later and pull them onto Mom's computer easily.

"You okay?" Mat asks, which makes me realize I'm tearing up.

I wipe at my eyes. "What do you mean?"

He gives me a stern look, so I drop my defenses.

"I like doing this. Baking, working on my coding

project, hanging out with you." I swallow, hard. "I think Mom would be happy that I'm doing this. I hate lying to Dad, but he just doesn't get it. He doesn't think I'm moving on with my life, but look at all the things I'm doing. I know I'm not, like, drowning in friends, but you . . ."

"I feel the same way, for what it's worth."

I reach out and grab his hand, tentatively, slowly, but I don't dare make eye contact. "It's worth a lot."

He holds my hand back for a few perfect seconds, but then that heavy look crosses his face again. He lets go, and my heart falls too.

"This has been such a perfect day." He sniffles. "I wanted to tell you earlier, but I . . . my mom . . . she's moving to Jersey temporarily. Like, *far* out. And she wants me to come with her."

"When?" I ask, my voice cracking.

He sighs. "Next week."

~~Mom's~~ Mat's "Perfect"
Chocolate Chip Cookie

INGREDIENTS

1 cup melted butter (that makes them crispy like Mat likes!)

1 cup sugar

1 cup brown sugar, packed (note: still don't know what packed means but the others tasted fine???)

1 tsp vanilla extract

2 eggs (I never want to see another egg again)

3 cups flour (note: it doesn't matter what color shirt you wear, you're getting covered in flour no matter what. Take a shower after to get it out of your ears.)

Baking soda, baking powder, and salt

1 1/2 cups chocolate chips

DIRECTIONS

Preheat oven to 375 degrees, spray a nonstick
baking sheet with cooking spray

Mix the dry ingredients in a large bowl, then
cream together the butter and sugar

Beat in vanilla then eggs one at a time

Mix in the dry ingredients SLOWLY

Stir in chocolate chips, then scoop the dough out
with a little ice cream scooper

Bake for 9 minutes exactly

Rest for a few minutes, then place cookies on a
cooling rack

CHEF'S TIP: If you eat the cookie too
soon, you'll burn the roof of your mouth. But . . .
sometimes it takes a little pain to find the joy.

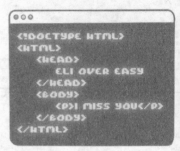

25

```
<!DOCTYPE HTML>
<HTML>
    <HEAD>
        ELI OVER EASY
    </HEAD>
    <BODY>
        <P>I MISS YOU</P>
    </BODY>
</HTML>
```

Mat leaves around four in the afternoon. He takes as many cookies as he can carry, leaving me with a dozen cookies that we cleverly placed in one of Mrs. Martinez's Tupperware, so I can tell Dad she made cookies for us. It was the only way to explain the smell of cookies everywhere, and I wanted to keep a few.

This time when Mat leaves, he takes my joy with him. I've made exactly one friend since moving to Manhattan (plus Mrs. Martinez, though I'm not sure if I can call someone almost sixty years older than me my friend), and even though I knew he was only here for the summer, I thought we had more time. I mean, it's only August!

I give the kitchen one more sweep, looking for any

crumbs of evidence revealing that I cooked (well, baked) while Dad was gone. I can't find any, so I plop onto the couch and release a sigh that feels like it'll never end.

So. One more week with Mat.

It's probably for the best anyway. I mean, Dad's been actively trying to get us back to Minnesota. Our friendship had an expiration date from the first time we met, me standing on a chair fanning the fire alarm after my first kitchen disaster.

I label all of the cookie photos and upload them to a site I created for the project, so I can just add a tag to pull up—[TooMuchSugar.png], for example—every time I reference the photos.

Tomorrow, I'm spending the whole day coding so I don't fall too far behind on this project. But today, I rest. And wallow a bit. And start to doze off on the couch . . .

I wake to the front door opening. Dad comes in and gives me a wave as he crosses to the living room.

"What's that smell?" he asks.

"Oh! Mrs. Martinez dropped off cookies. I may have eaten a few . . . okay, more than a few, already."

He sniffs around, then opens the Tupperware and

takes out a cookie. He eats it quickly, and from the look on his face, it's clear he's into it.

"Do you prefer chewier cookies or crunchier cookies?" I ask. "Mat likes them crunchy."

"I think these are perfect," he says, then briefly tacks on, "just like the ones your mom made."

I keep an even expression, even though I'm kind of flipping out inside—first off, I must have nailed the recipe. But second, this might be the first time he's just casually mentioned Mom in conversation without getting weird.

"Can we talk?" he asks, and he comes around to sit in the chair near me.

That's never a good thing, I think.

"Sure," I say.

"I . . ." He looks away. "You know what, never mind."

Part of me feels relieved, but the other part feels unexpectedly disappointed. I realize then how much I've craved a real conversation with my dad about everything that's been going on.

I mean, we're all we've got.

He stands and walks into the kitchen to grab another cookie, and a perplexed expression takes over his face. He looks to me again, half smiles, and says the last words I ever expected to come out of his mouth.

"Do you want to cook together today?" he asks. "I can make my fajitas."

I smile and nod. Even though I'm exhausted from cooking all day, and I need to focus on my coding work, I can't pass up a chance like this.

"That sounds great," I say. "I forgot you used to make those all the time in Minnesota."

He eyes me suspiciously, though I honestly don't understand why. "You forgot?"

"Yeah . . . ?" I shrug.

He doesn't elaborate. "Interesting."

We grab a reusable grocery bag and some cash and make our way downstairs. Outside the apartment building, the late afternoon sun is blinding. I look down the street to see the Empire State Building glisten, and despite the heat and my mixed-up feelings about Mat, I smile.

"Ann usually has better produce than they have outside the bodega," I say, gesturing at the vegetable cart vendor across the street. "Oh, but she still doesn't know about Mom."

"She knew Mom?" Dad asks as I pull him across the street.

"Yeah, that's where Mom got all her produce. Ann talked to me about her once, but I didn't know what to say." I slow to a stop. "I still don't."

"Eli!" Ann yells. "It's been a while. You haven't been cooking much lately?"

"Not lately." I give a side-eye to Dad. "But we're making fajitas tonight, and those huge peppers look great. Dad, what do we usually get?"

"Oh, uh," he stutters, "just an onion, a red pepper, and a green one."

"Here," she says, getting up from her stool and walking around to her veggies. "It's late in the day, but we still have some good-looking ones."

She drops the veggies in the bag quickly; a bright flash of green and yellow and red fly into the bag.

"Oh, we don't need a yellow," he says, but she just shakes her head.

"It's on the house, no worries. The yellow ones are sweeter, you'll love them." She pauses. "That'll be . . . three dollars."

"But it's two fifty per pepper," Dad says.

"Don't argue with her," I say, and she laughs.

"Just like your son, and just like your wife. You're all good people, you get a discount." She winks.

"Thanks so much," I say.

We say our goodbyes, and I lead Dad back toward the corner store. "Sorry, I don't know how to tell her about Mom."

"I wouldn't either," he replies, a little bewildered. "Couldn't we stop by the bodega for the rest?"

"Mrs. Martinez always gets her chicken from the corner store up here. They're great too." I pause. "I don't think our bodega even has chicken."

He laughs. "I kind of figured they had everything."

We pop into the store, and the owner greets us as we walk in. "Hey, you're that kid who comes in with Mrs. Martinez sometimes, right?"

"You just get recognized by everyone, don't you?" Dad asks.

I blush and nod.

"She called me yesterday to make sure I held on to the best-looking steak that came in today's shipment, but she hasn't been in to get it yet. Could you bring it over to her?" he says. "She can pay me next time she's in, I know she's good for it."

"Oh, sure," I say.

Dad and I shop for the rest of the ingredients and toppings, including the chicken, some seasonings, flour tortillas, cheese, refried beans, and a packet of quick-cook Mexican rice.

"Please tell me you don't get a discount here too," Dad says.

I laugh. "No, that's just with Ann."

We finish up shopping, pay, and head back toward the house. It must be Embarrass Eli Day because on our way back, we pass by the bodega owner, who's smoking outside. He calls me Egg Boy again and gives us a hard time about shopping at his competitor.

I roll my eyes. "I promise, I only get my eggs from you."

"That I like to hear," he says with a smirk on his face.

Finally, after it feels like I've been flagged down by the whole neighborhood, we make it back to the apartment. As Dad unpacks, I run the steak over to Mrs. Martinez's apartment. She doesn't answer, so I shoot Mat a text to let him know it's in our fridge.

When I come back, Dad inspects a slightly greasy baking sheet closely, and I pray that Mat did a good enough job cleaning it that my cover isn't busted. Dad sets it down without a word, though.

We wash our hands, and for the first time in ages, we cook a dinner from scratch together.

26

```
<!DOCTYPE HTML>
<HTML>
    <HEAD>
        ELI OVER EASY
    </HEAD>
    <BODY>
        <P>I MISS YOU</P>
    </BODY>
</HTML>
```

"**I**'m about to throw my computer out the window," I tell Riley on the phone the next day. "But it's one hundred and two degrees today, so I'm pretty sure opening the window would instantly incinerate me."

"At least you've got your priorities straight," she says. "What's going on? I don't know anything about coding, but maybe I can help?"

I grit my teeth and hit the return key harder than I should.

"It's not working, none of it is working."

"Do you want to reach out to your professor?"

I shake my head. "He's out of the office today for a long weekend. I don't know why he'd go on vacation right before asking us to turn in our biggest project, but I just have to figure it out myself."

"Hmm . . . do you know anyone else in the class? Maybe they could help?"

"I don't need their help," I say.

There's silence on the other end. "Is this one of those things where you just need to vent? If you're not looking for a solution, that's fine, vent away. I just want to make sure I know what I'm in for with this chat."

"I'm just venting. I think I can figure it out, it's just . . . hard." I sigh. "I can't believe I voluntarily took on two projects. I couldn't just do the recipe generator or the cookie troubleshooter, I had to do *both*. And currently, I'm doing neither correctly."

"You'll get through it, babe," she says kindly. "Hey, how were those fajitas? That pic you sent me looked so good."

"Now, *that* went well. It's been forever since I cooked with Dad, and he even suggested it. He was kind of weird about it at the beginning, but it ended up being fun. Maybe we're over the whole awkwardness from before."

"I hope so!" Riley says. "Maybe he'll let you cook more. I still think you should stream it. It would be such a fun show."

I shrug. "Maybe. It would be kind of fun, like I'm putting my own spin on what Mom did with her You-Tube videos."

"Do you think . . ." She stops. "Don't get mad, okay, but do you think your dad was a little bit right about you cooking just because you miss your mom? I don't think it's bad, even if it's true. I've just been thinking about it recently, and I see his point."

"I don't know," I reply honestly. "I do like cooking. Way more than I thought I would. But what if Dad's right, and I'm just stuck in the past? What am I going to do after I watch Mom's last two videos?"

"Well, *I* hope you keep cooking. You can make your own recipes, even!"

"Yeah," I say with a laugh. "And test them out in front of a ton of strangers on the internet while they all make fun of me. Oh, hey, how's that been going for you?"

"You mean that guy who was harassing me? Well, I may have gotten his channel temporarily banned." She laughs not so innocently. "That'll teach anyone to cross me. Plus, the streaming service passed along some tips on how to prevent nasty comments in the future. Being a girl in the gaming world just comes with this kind of stuff, but that doesn't mean I have to put up with it!"

"Good! He deserves a permanent ban, but hopefully he thinks twice before crossing you."

"His little stunt got me five *hundred* new followers. And a few paid subscribers too. So thanks for the money, hope he enjoys streaming jail!"

Eventually, I tell her I have to get off the phone so I can get back to my project. I skim some JavaScript videos, revisit past assignments, watch YouTube tutorials, and do anything else I can to figure this out.

I shoot Mat another text once I realize he never got back to me about the steak in our fridge.

The more I research, the more frustrated I get. The recipe generator should be working. I can click through and tell it I like crispy cookies, dense cookies, whatever, and I still get the same result: a PDF with some truly bizarre, unreadable code all over it.

I go to warm up some leftovers, and that's when I realize the chicken paprikash is gone from the fridge. Did Dad throw it out? Or did he eat it? I feel the anxiety creep into my chest, hoping it was the latter . . . but knowing it was the former. Sure, he was great about making fajitas, which is *his* thing. But the second anything comes up that reminds him of Mom, it's gone—in the trash.

I heat up leftover fajitas all while scrolling through lines and lines of code. I should take a break. My head's throbbing with how much I'm squinting at the screen, and I'm getting so frustrated that I need to take deep, deep breaths to keep my cool.

I assemble my fajitas, grab a Dr Pepper, and decide to put on one of Riley's horror streams. I turn the volume down, since I know she's going to be screaming a *lot*.

The horror game Riley's streaming isn't very gruesome, but it's full of jump scares. It's not my kind of game, but watching her navigate the maze of traps and scares is so fascinating that I get wrapped up in it anyway.

Riley's character walks slowly down a pitch-black hallway, and I can hear the sobs of fear coming from her. Her character has an injured leg from an earlier zombie attack, and she's inching closer and closer to a door. The chat starts getting hyped, and I realize they know exactly what's behind the door, but Riley has no idea.

Her hand reaches out for the doorknob, painfully slowly.

Knock! Knock! Knock!

I scream, dropping my fajita on the ground. *That* sound was in real life. I hastily pause the stream and pick up my mess, then cross over to the door. Though I'd normally forego my dad's advice and open the door, I'm a little jumpy from watching the stream, so I take out the step stool, peer slowly into the peephole.

I sigh. It's just Mat, so I fling open the door.

"Did you just scream?" he asks.

I wrap him in a quick hug. "I'm so glad you're not a zombie."

"You . . . what?"

"Never mind. Come in. Do you want some leftover fajitas? Dad and I cooked together last night, totally unprompted, I—"

I hold the door open, but he won't cross through the threshold. He's looking down, a sad expression across his face.

"Everything okay?" I ask.

He shakes his head. "My grandma's sick. She's been at the hospital all night."

"Oh no!" I say. "What happened?"

"When I got back yesterday, she could barely get out of bed. Apparently she was feeling dizzy all day, but was too stubborn to go to the doctor. I . . . I really screwed up."

"Mat . . ." I say, the flash of hospitals, doctors, beeping machines flooding my brain. "Is she gonna be okay?"

He nods. "The doctors say she'll be okay. It's a kidney infection. She wants to come home already but the doctors won't let her."

"That sounds like her," I say softly.

"I should have been there, Eli."

I give him a confused look.

"I wasn't there. She spent all day in pain, and I was over here making cookies!" He sighs. "I was supposed to watch her."

"I'm sorry I—"

"I'm not blaming you. I'm blaming *me*." He shakes his head. "I know I'm only here for another six days, but I need to take this job seriously."

"Didn't you say that you watching her was something your parents made up, so they could . . . figure things out?"

"I guess I was wrong. She needed help, and she didn't get it. But anyway, I wanted to get that steak from you, and then I have to go clean the apartment and make sure everything is perfect for her. She might get discharged tonight, but she'll need a lot of help while I'm still here."

I nod. "Want a hand?"

"No, it's okay."

His voice is cold, and I feel tears well up in my eyes. I turn to the fridge and pass him the slab of meat the corner store guy gave me.

"Let me know if you need me, okay?" I finally say.

He doesn't make eye contact, but he nods. I slowly shut the door, and realize I'd have preferred zombies to that news.

Mrs. Martinez seemed so strong just two days ago. But then again, I know how quickly things can turn from okay to bad. *Real* bad.

I take my time cleaning up my fajita mess. I turn off the stream completely. I pace back and forth. My legs are sluggish but my brain is on fire.

Hospital gowns.

Doctors.

Beeping.

I'm cold. It's over a hundred degrees outside, but I start to shiver. I lie on the couch and pull a blanket over me, and as I look at my computer, the tears start to blur the lines of broken, useless code on the screen.

I try to hold my grief in, like I did when Dad told me the news. When we went to the funeral. When I returned to school as the kid whose mom just died. But I can't anymore. I curl up into a ball and get my phone out to send Dad a text.

Can you come home?

27

```
<!DOCTYPE HTML>
<HTML>
    <HEAD>
        ELI OVER EASY
    </HEAD>
    <BODY>
        <P>I MISS YOU</P>
    </BODY>
</HTML>
```

"Eli?" Dad says softly after opening the front door and finding me balled up on the couch. "How are you under that blanket? It's burning up."

I shrug, though I'm not sure he can see my movement. I reach for my glasses and put them on, and he comes into view.

"What's going on?" he asks.

He's calmer than usual, and that surprises me. Since Mom died, he's been a frantic mess. His worry for me has been a little overbearing at times too. But this is different. He's alert, focused, in control.

I sigh, long and slow, and start to sit upright, pushing the blanket off me. I'm a little dizzy, but I run a hand through my hair.

"Sorry to make you come home from work early," I say. "Mrs. Martinez, she's . . . in the hospital."

"Oh god—is she okay?"

I nod. "Kidney infection. She'll just need to rest some, but Mat's pretty upset."

"And you?"

"I don't know. Once Mat left, I just kept thinking back to the hospital. The beeping, the masks, the sanitary smell."

He sits next to me and pulls me into a tight hug, and I relax into him.

"I thought I was getting better. The cooking, it . . . it really did help. Or I thought it did." I let out a whimper. "But I guess you were right."

"No, I wasn't right. Cooking with you yesterday was the most fun I've had around here in a while. I was just watching you cut the veggies, and you knew exactly what you were doing. It's . . . wild. You seemed happy."

"I like cooking," I say. "I mean, I don't think I want it to be my career, but it's fun. But what if it is making me miss Mom more? What if I'm just clinging to this because—"

"It's okay to cling to this, I think," he says, releasing me from his hug and giving me a smile. "Cooking is something you'll always have to remind you of your mom. A happy thing to remind you of her, that is. Not like this hospital business."

"I feel so selfish," I say. "I'm making this all about me."

"We went through so much with Mom's passing. You can't just get over that. There are going to be things that, for lack of a better word, trigger bad memories like this. I'm not a therapist or anything, but I think that might not be a bad thing. Hopefully it gets better, someday."

"And if it doesn't?" I ask.

"It will," he says. "You know I have my rough moments too. So why don't we get ahead of it for the next time something like this happens. I'll do some research on therapists and we'll find one you like."

"Okay." I clear my throat. "For what it's worth, I think . . . I think I'm getting closer to Mom, in a way, through all this cooking. That's why I don't want to stop. That's why . . ."

"That's why you made the chicken paprikash? Which was fantastic, by the way."

"You ate it?"

He nods. "Sorry I wasn't more supportive earlier.

We'll call that one of *my* rough moments. That . . . that was the first dish your mom ever made me. Weird how memories get you sometimes."

I hug Dad again and let a few more tears escape onto his button-down shirt.

"Anyway, I think we'd all feel better if we did something to help Mrs. Martinez. Do you know what Mom would do in this situation?"

I laugh. "Cook something?"

"Bingo." He winks. "Is she back from the hospital yet?"

"I think she's coming back tonight."

He snaps his fingers. "You know, there was that one breakfast casserole Mom used to make, where she'd prep everything the night before, let it sit in the fridge overnight, then bake it in the morning. I bet Mrs. Martinez and Mat would love to wake up and have a hot breakfast ready for them."

"I'll find a recipe!" I say, grabbing my computer. "And I'll let Mat know not to worry about breakfast tomorrow. Wait, tomorrow's Friday—don't you have work? Are you going to let me bake it myself?"

He laughs. "I would let you bake it yourself, but I'm actually not going in tomorrow. I have a Zoom interview that is *much* more promising than that last one."

I smile, but inside I'm aching. I keep forgetting that, through all of this, Dad's been actively trying to get a remote job so he can move us back to Minneapolis. And I guess, with Mat leaving too, I don't have much to stay for.

But, besides Mat, there are so many things I'll miss about living here.

The rest of the afternoon is taken up by researching recipes, shopping for ingredients, chopping and prepping everything for Mrs. Martinez's breakfast casserole. Unfortunately, the day was such a mess that I didn't get any more progress done on my coding project.

I only have a few days left to turn it in, so I take the laptop into my room before bed to try to troubleshoot what's going on. But almost immediately, my headache returns. I decide I can't use my brain tonight.

Without putting too much thought into it, I click into Mom's YouTube page. *Renee's Test Kitchen* only has three videos that I haven't seen. I'm not sure I'm ready for the series to end, but I miss her so much right now that I can't help myself.

This time, though, I don't take notes. I don't try to

decipher the recipe. I just watch Mom in her kitchen, fully in her element, as she cooks Hungarian cabbage rolls. Immediately, I'm hit with a wave of nostalgia—I can smell the vinegary sauerkraut, the sweet stewed tomatoes, and the warmth of the paprika-doused ground sausage. Maybe I'll try this recipe one day, but right now, I watch her video like it was a true cooking show.

And after it's done, my heart feels a little more whole.

Eli & Dad's Breakfast Casserole

INGREDIENTS

Frozen hash browns (the shredded kind NOT

the little potato cubes!!!)

A tube of sausage (is that an official

measurement??)

Onion & bell pepper diced

2 cups (a whole bag) shredded cheddar cheese

10 eggs (still keeping the egg industry alive)

A cup of whole milk

Salt (plus whatever spices Dad decides to

throw in there)

DIRECTIONS

PREHEAT OVEN (future Eli: DO NOT

FORGET—preheating is *important*!!)

Cook the sausage, peppers, and onions (I'll do

the ~~chopping~~ DICING and let dad do that)

Grease a casserole dish (dad just rubs a
stick of butter all over it) and layer frozen
hashbrowns, sausage, veggies, and most of the
cheese

LEAVE SOME CHEESE TO TOP

Whisk up all those eggs (note: I need to lay off
the eggs, this is too much) with milk, salt, spices,
then pour it evenly into the casserole dish, top
with the rest of the cheese

note: we'll let it sit in the fridge overnight and
bake it in the morning fresh for Mrs. Martinez!

Bake for an hour or so

CHEF'S TIP: Dad says Mom always said
cooking with someone, or cooking for someone, is
the best way to make someone feel better.

28

```
<!DOCTYPE HTML>
<HTML>
   <HEAD>
      ELI OVER EASY
   </HEAD>
   <BODY>
      <P>I MISS YOU</P>
   </BODY>
</HTML>
```

sleep in. Even though I went to bed feeling pretty good, the next morning, it's almost impossible to get out from under the covers. I'm exhausted physically, but mentally too. Cooking with Dad, thinking about Mom all night—it's a lot. Healing is . . . definitely not a straight line.

Eventually, the thing that gets me up is a text from Mat with an update about his grandma. Thankfully, she's feeling okay and is still sleeping after getting in late last night. He says we can bring over the casserole whenever, but I know it takes an hour to bake, so I jump out of bed and rush to my door.

But when I open it, the smell of eggs, sausage, and peppers hits my nose.

"Morning," Dad says. "Got a head start on the baking. Hope you don't mind. How are you feeling?"

"Really crappy, actually," I say, and Dad laughs.

"Sorry, I didn't mean to laugh. Guess I'm not used to us being so honest with each other."

"When's your interview?" I ask.

"In about an hour. This will be done in thirty. We'll let it cool, and then I thought you could take it over while I have my interview." He sighs. "I need to shower, shave, and get into a suit. Think you got this from here?"

I smile. "I'm on it!"

I pour myself a glass of orange juice and settle into the couch. I pull up Riley's video on from yesterday and turn the volume down, so her screams don't terrify the whole building. While I watch the recording of Riley screaming her brains out while the zombies *eat* her brains, I send her a quick series of texts to update her on everything that happened yesterday.

Once that's done, I go back into coding land, making small adjustments to both pieces to see if I can get anything to work. My brain's still a little foggy, but I do catch a few issues right away. I make a few taps, expecting the custom recipe app to work flawlessly.

It . . . does not.

Same garbage error messages I can't understand.

I groan and spend the next thirty minutes scouring for bugs, lines of bad code, or anything that would explain the issue, but I find nothing. And suddenly, it's already time to take out the casserole.

Reaching into the oven with my gloved hand, I get a huge whiff of the casserole, and I start drooling immediately. I let it rest on the stovetop and let Mat know I'll be over in fifteen, then text back and forth with Riley for a bit.

She tells me to enjoy her latest video because she's going offline for the next week. A mental health hiatus, she's calling it. I'm not sure what she'll do with all her free time, but I don't challenge it. It's clear I don't know how anything works, mental-health-wise.

"God, that smells great," Dad says, coming into the room while adjusting his tie. "I'll hop over there with you, just to say hello, then I'll come back for my interview."

I grab a handful of forks, plates, and serving utensils while Dad carries the casserole dish. We make our way to Mrs. Martinez's apartment, and Mat answers almost as soon as I knock.

He throws his arms around me. "Eli."

"Mat," I say, blushing. "I would hug you back, but I think I'd poke you with all these forks."

He laughs. "Fair. Come in, that smells fantastic."

There's a part of me that expects Mrs. Martinez to look like my mom did, at the end. After all, I've seen what a short amount of time in a hospital can do to someone. But she looks as strong as ever. She gives us a kind smile as we walk in, and claps her hands together when Dad places the casserole dish on a trivet on her coffee table.

"Oh, this looks just perfect," she says. "You didn't have to go to all this trouble."

"It's nothing," Dad says. "We like doing it, and you shouldn't have to worry about meals while you're recovering."

Dad ducks out to go to his Zoom interview while I serve everyone a slice of the casserole.

"Ooh, hash browns are *in* the casserole?" Mat says with wonder. "Yum."

The rest of our conversation is light, though it's clear Mat's still a little shaken by the situation. He sits close to his grandma, and jumps up to get her water, hot sauce, anything she needs as soon as she needs it.

She starts to get up, but Mat stops her.

"Let me do it," he says.

"Mathias, I have to pee," she says sternly. "Are you going to pee for me?"

He blushes.

"That's what I thought." She gives me a wink. "Now excuse me."

She gets up and walks, slowly, toward the back of the apartment.

"Hey, are you okay?" I ask. "I know that really shook you."

"I don't know. Grandma told me it wasn't my fault. My mom told me it wasn't my fault. But I still feel so bad."

"I'm sorry," I say. "I'm sorry if I was taking up too much of your time or something. I distracted you so I could do this cooking thing, just to feel a little closer to my mom, but . . ."

I laugh, and he gives me a strange stare.

"I had the most spectacular breakdown yesterday. It was . . . a long time coming, I guess. I'm still trying to figure out how much of this cooking stuff was a cry for help and how much of it was therapy. Maybe it was both."

Mat reaches across the table, and instinctively I give him my hand. It's not exactly comfortable, or particularly romantic, but something unspoken goes through us. He's here for me, and I'm here for him.

"I wish you didn't have to go," I eventually say.

"I wish I didn't either. Mom's coming over tonight, and I think she's going to stay with us for a few days while Grandma gets back on her feet."

"I'm already on my feet!" she snaps as she returns from the restroom.

We release each other's hands, and I laugh nervously.

The conversation stays significantly lighter for the rest of breakfast. I talk to Mat about Riley's horror stream, and he tries to convince me again to start streaming my cooking.

"I think your mom would like that," Mrs. Martinez says. "You'd be doing just what she did, but . . . a young person's take on it. Does your father still not know about these videos?"

I look down. "I haven't told him, no. I will soon, but I think I want to watch the rest of them before I do. What if he gets upset and tells me to stop watching them?"

Mat laughs. "If he did that, you'd probably still find a way to watch them. Plus, he wouldn't do that. You just said how you've been more honest with each other, right?"

"Mm-hmm," I grumble.

"Maybe you can be honest with him about this too."

After our chat, I gather up the plates as Mat wraps the casserole in aluminum foil. Dad was very clear that we don't need the dish back until they've finished it off. Mat opens the door for me, and I give him a quick, one-armed hug.

"Sorry," I say with a smirk. "Midwest habit."

"Sure." He returns my smile. "Bye, Eli."

Back in our apartment, I quietly place the dishes in the sink and creep over to Dad's bedroom to see if he's still on his call. I can't hear him talking, which briefly makes me worried that he's sitting in there quietly.

But then the door opens, and I stumble through.

"Can I help you?" he asks with a grin on his face.

"I wasn't sure if your interview was over!"

"It is, and it went *fantastic*."

I give him a quick hug. My smile is genuine, but I'd be lying if I said I wasn't still torn. I want him to get this job, but I don't know if I'm ready to move back to Minneapolis.

"Want to go out to lunch to celebrate?" he asks.

I hesitate. "I . . . have to finish my coding project.

It's still not working, and I don't know how long it will take."

"Oh, right!" he says, showing no signs of disappointment. "That takes priority. Good luck. I'm going to go take a walk and tell the news to Aunt Chloe. I feel good about this one!"

He grabs his phone and keys and walks out the door, and I try to wipe the dumbstruck look off my face. Just a few weeks ago, Dad was a recluse, king of the hermits, but today he wants to take a walk and call Aunt Chloe? Maybe our little honesty session helped us both after all.

My high spirits die as soon as I open my computer. The code intimidates me; it doesn't make any sense. But I try anyway.

Hours pass and I don't have much progress to show for it. I fixed a few more bugs, and the code is pulling up a full recipe—finally—but something's wrong with the personalization. It's like it can't remember all of the choices, so it randomly assigns recipes at the end, Frankenstein ones with no flour and extra eggs.

I'm not sure if this is better or worse than it was when I started. It's still messed up, just differently. I keep working as the sun fades from my bedroom window. Dad throws together a quick dinner of pasta and jarred tomato sauce and brings it to my room.

"You've been working at this a *lot*. I wish I could help. Do . . . do you want me to run it past some of the developers I work with? I'm sure they could give it a look."

"No, I want to fix it myself . . . besides, I have to turn it in Monday morning. Not sure your developers would be too happy to work for you on the weekend."

"You're right about that." He chuckles. "Well, don't be up too late. Let me know if you need me, okay?"

"Will do," I say shortly, and I feel the fatigue claw at my brain.

I put on another "lo-fi beats to study to" video on YouTube and drill back into my work, toggling between making small tweaks to the code and googling everything I can about the coding issues I'm having. When the video ends, five hours later, it's late, and I'm so much closer on both projects.

But . . . it's still wrong.

It's all wrong.

29

```
<!DOCTYPE HTML>
<HTML>
    <HEAD>
        ELI OVER EASY
    </HEAD>
    <BODY>
        <P>I MISS YOU</P>
    </BODY>
</HTML>
```

Dad and I sit at the bagel shop on Sunday morning with our laptops. He's catching up on some work that he missed on Friday, and I'm turning in my coding project one day early. Even though it is still completely broken.

When I first woke up today, I felt a little bit of hope that I'd have a breakthrough. But I'd stared at the code so much, it started looking like it was written in a foreign language. I couldn't debug it anymore. I couldn't even *look* at it anymore.

And that's when I decided to turn it in as is.

Mr. Parker,

I've attached my projects to this document.

As you'll see, neither of them work like they're

supposed to. I've gone through the code hundreds of times, and I was able to fix so many of the mistakes that I found—I made notes about them within the code as I fixed them—but in the end, you were right. I should have focused all my energy on either the recipe generator or the cookie troubleshooter. Instead, I thought I could take on both, and now you have two broken apps to grade. I'm sorry.

Eli

"There," I say. "I turned it in."

"Congrats!" Dad shouts. "Do you want a celebratory second bagel?"

I shake my head. "Believe me, I don't deserve it. I've spent all week, all weekend, trying to make this app work, but it just . . . doesn't. I hope he gives me partial credit or something. I know this doesn't end up on my report card or anything, but I really wanted to ace this class."

"Eli, you deserve it. You've learned so much in so little time."

I sigh, then smile. "You know what, screw it. I do deserve a second bagel."

Dad goes up and orders a cinnamon raisin bagel with cream cheese, and we split it when he comes back. We start to pack up and go, but then I notice Ann, who runs the veggie cart, is at a table by herself in the back. She gives us a kind wave, which I return.

"Dad, wait." I whisper. "I think I should tell her about Mom. She's stopped asking about her, but Mom liked Ann, and it only seems fair."

He looks at me and nods. "Okay. Want me to come with you?"

I shake my head.

I take the few steps over to her and slide into the chair across from her. She gives me a cheery smile and asks me how I've been.

"Good," I say. "I wanted to tell you something. I know I've been acting weird about my mom every time you bring her up. And . . . it's just . . . she passed away a few months ago. I wasn't sure how to tell you."

She gives me a sad smile. "Thank you for telling me. Mrs. Martinez finally told me all about it a few weeks ago, and I felt so bad that I kept asking about her. She was a sweet person."

"Oh, I'm glad you knew," I say. "Sorry I didn't tell you right away."

She reaches over and places a hand over mine.

"She was one of my favorite customers, and now you are too." She winks. "I'm looking out for you, okay? I'll set aside the best produce for you."

I laugh, and I promise to swing by this week to pick up some groceries. Then I leave her to eat her bagel in peace, and rejoin my dad. He just puts an arm on my shoulder as we leave the bagel shop.

As we approach the front door to the apartment building, Mat's on his way out.

"Oh, Eli!" he says.

"Mat!" I say with a smile.

"I'm going to pick up some things at the pharmacy for my grandma. Want to come with?" he asks, then turns to my dad. "If that's okay, Mr. Adams."

I turn to Dad, expecting him to say no. Considering how he felt the need to show me how to lock the door eight times before he left me alone his first day back in the office, and how Mrs. Martinez was concerned I was one of those leash kids, I don't have a lot of hope for this moment.

But he barely hesitates. "Sure! Here, let me take your laptop upstairs, and let me give you some cash so you can buy a couple candy bars for the two of you."

"O . . . kay," I say. "Thanks, Dad."

Mat and I walk up the street toward the Empire State Building, where there's a Duane Reade a couple blocks away. We don't say much, but our shoulders touch sometimes as we walk. After a little hesitation, he takes my hand in his.

This . . . isn't something I ever thought I'd be comfortable doing in front of so many people. But the thing about New York City is that, even though you're surrounded by thousands of people everywhere you go, it feels like you're alone.

When Mom died, I'd just look out at the window as hundreds of people walked by. Even though I was stuck, life moved on for everyone else. I felt alone and insignificant, but also a little inspired. And every time I'm around these people, it feels like we're alone together.

We're all on our own paths, but New York City propels us forward, so we're always changing, always moving. And even though Mat and I will be going down different paths soon, for this one beautiful moment, we're not alone.

We pull on our masks and go into the pharmacy, the wave of air-conditioning instantly chilling me on this toasty day. I grab us a few candy bars while Mat picks up his grandma's prescription, and we meander around together.

"Mom says we're leaving on Wednesday," Mat finally says. "My aunt's got a place out in Jersey that we can crash at."

"What about your home up in Yonkers?"

"Dad's going to stay there. He said I could stay whenever I wanted, and they'd have a bed for me." He sighs. "I hate this."

"I'm sorry, Mat."

We leave the pharmacy and walk down the street to a bench outside a grab-and-go coffee shop. He swings his feet as he sits, which is kind of cute, while we eat candy bars and watch the people, dogs, and even one turtle walk by.

"I want to stay here," he says. "With my grandma. At least until they figure things out. I know it doesn't make sense, and it's not that I don't want to be with my parents, but . . . she actually does need help. And what if this happens again and she's too stubborn to go to the doctor and we're all so far away?"

"I could check on her," I say. "Dad can too. That is, until we go back to Minnesota."

"Crap, you're really going to go back?"

I nod. "Dad feels great about this interview he just had. I don't know if we'd be moving overnight—I don't think apartments let you do that—but I don't know. My days here feel . . . numbered."

"This is such a cool place to live," Mat says, and I nod. "Oh, hey, how'd your project go?"

"It's . . . as good as I could get it," I say. "And by that, I mean it's still broken."

He laughs. "Do you have any more time to fix it?"

"No, I turned it in already. I couldn't even look at the screen without getting a headache." I shrug. "So I'll fail the coding boot camp I begged my parents to put me into for the last three years."

"You showed me the code, and it was some of the most confusing stuff I've ever seen. Like, you type in a complete mess of letters and brackets and numbers and somehow there are pictures of cookies on the screen. Are you kidding me?" He laughs. "It's magic."

"Broken magic," I say. "But thanks. Even though it didn't go as well as I planned, I guess I learned a lot."

"So, can we hang out tomorrow? And the next day? And . . . well, the next day, if I'm still here?"

I laugh. "Definitely. Maybe Dad will even let us cook!"

On cue, Dad sends me a text.

Hey, everything okay? Totally fine if you're still out. Just making sure you're okay. Sorry. See you soon.

"Yeah . . . we'll see about that," I say, showing Mat the text.

He laughs, and we make our way back to the apartment, hand in hand.

30

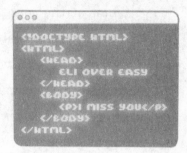

```
<!DOCTYPE HTML>
<HTML>
    <HEAD>
        ELI OVER EASY
    </HEAD>
    <BODY>
        <P>I MISS YOU</P>
    </BODY>
</HTML>
```

The next morning, I wake after the first truly restful night in days. Saying goodbye to that coding project was exactly what I needed just to let my brain relax.

I go out into the living room, but as soon as I open the door, the smell of bacon smacks me in the face. Dad's making *breakfast*?

"Shouldn't you be getting ready for work?" I ask, noticing that he's still in the T-shirt and shorts he usually sleeps in.

He points the spatula at me. "No work today."

"Oh?" I say. "Is it a holiday, or . . ."

"I took some vacation leave this week to celebrate the end of your coding classes . . . and also because I hate my job."

I laugh. "Makes sense to me."

"I have a few surprises planned, but first, bacon."

I sit at the counter on a bar stool, and Dad presents me with a plate of fried eggs, bacon, and toast. He passes me strawberry jelly, followed by a glass of orange juice. I sit patiently while he finishes cooking his eggs, makes his plate, and pours himself a giant mug of coffee.

We sit next to each other, not saying much but digging into this incredible breakfast.

"You never made breakfast," I say.

He laughs. "I used to! Back when you were real young, I made breakfast every day, because your mom was working late nights at that restaurant. Once her schedule got a little better, and mine got a little worse, we'd alternate, until eventually she just made breakfast every day."

"I guess you're Egg Boy now," I say, which makes Dad laugh.

"You know, the bodega owner made the exact same joke this morning."

We eat our breakfast, and I try to get any details about the surprises of the day. The only thing Dad says is that he's positive I'll like it. After I take my last bite of eggs, my phone buzzes in my pocket.

I pull it out and see an email from my professor show up on my lock screen.

"Oh no." I groan. "My coding teacher responded."

Dad stays silent while I read the email:

Eli,

Don't be so hard on yourself. I've taken a look through all of your changes, and I think you've done a spectacular job troubleshooting the errors. There are plenty of things that we never went over in class in here, and the code is clean, which shows me that you grasp this. You have a talent for coding, and for researching, and apparently, for baking cookies too! I hate to tell you this, because it's going to make you a little upset . . . but in the end, if you close the brackets in line 36 and 530, the code works. Completely. You fixed all of the major issues on your own, which is some brilliant work, but like I told you, even the most experienced coders make these kinds of mistakes.

I've adjusted the code and uploaded everything to our server. Your web app is on display along with all of the others from our class . . . but you'll notice that yours is by far the most complex. Don't beat yourself up over this. You've become a brilliant coder, and I hope you continue to pursue it.

It's been a pleasure teaching you, and it probably goes without saying, but you're approved for the coding boot camp certificate, which should come in the mail in the next two weeks. Congrats, Eli.

All my best,
Mr. Parker

"Holy crap," I say, clicking into the web app and tapping a few buttons. "It works, it all works!"

"He fixed it?" Dad asks. "Can I see?"

I hesitate since I never confessed about lying to him about the cookies. But he needs to know, and a part of me wants to show it off. So, semi-reluctantly, I open the app and pass my phone over to him.

"So." I clear my throat. "The app has two functions, you can pick."

"Let's see . . ." He taps the phone. "Oh, *interesting*. Let me find my perfect chocolate chip cookie recipe."

The survey opens, and he taps a few selections. It turns out, he likes his cookies like I do, a little chewier, balanced sweetness, with a buttery taste.

"When you tap 'Get Your Recipe,' it should pull up a personalized recipe."

He does, and after a second of loading, a PDF takes over my phone with a full cookie recipe.

"Does it say to refrigerate the dough?" I ask since that's the key to chewy cookies.

"It does!" he says in awe. "So if I made these cookies, they'd be exactly what I want?"

I nod. "Mat likes thin and crispy cookies, so his ingredients list would say melted butter. Riley said she likes them packed with chocolate chips, so that would adjust the amount for her and tweak the ratio so that they still bake well. I want to update it in the future to include, like, gluten-free or dairy-free substitutions too."

"This is so cool," he says, going back to the home page and into the cookie troubleshooting tool. "And what's this?"

"So that is everything that could be wrong with your cookies. So if you make cookies but don't understand why they're too cakey, you'd tap this photo here . . . and it says that you either left out baking soda or maybe your baking soda has expired."

As I show him, my smile grows. Fine, I missed a

couple brackets, but I did this. I married my love of coding with Mom's cooking tips and made *Renee's Test Kitchen* an app. Sort of.

"And where did you get all these pictures?" he asks smoothly, though he must have put it together by now.

"Mat and I took them ourselves. I . . . I baked all of those." I sigh.

"Yeah . . . I kind of figured, once I came home and the entire apartment smelled like freshly baked cookies." He laughs. "A Tupperware alone can't do that. Oh, and when I made those fajitas, there were still cookie-shaped grease rings on the baking sheet. That confirmed my suspicions."

I cringe. "Sorry for keeping everything from you."

"Thanks for saying that. I know we went through a little rough patch there, but could you promise not to lie to me like that again?" He sighs. "I know I can't keep track of everything you're doing, and I was being a little controlling about the cooking. But it freaked me out that you lied to my face so easily."

"It wasn't easy," I say with a long sigh, "but yeah. I promise."

"But you *really* didn't understand why I suggested

fajitas that night?" he asks.

I give him an odd look. "Um, no. Why would I?"

"In the last two months, you cooked eggs, rice, chicken paprikash, chocolate chip cookies . . ." he says, his voice drifting off. "Did you not watch them all?"

My cheeks flush red as it dawns on me—he knows about the videos. He's known all this time?!

"Watch . . . what?" I say, mumbling the words.

I avoid eye contact in embarrassment as I realize that he's not only known about the videos, but he's known about all my cooking—and my *reasons* for cooking—ever since fajita night.

"Take a look at episode six," is all he says. "I'm going to take a shower. Then we have to clean up this mess so we can start our adventure."

He leaves me in stunned silence. Once he closes his bedroom door, I scramble back to my room and open my laptop, go to Mom's YouTube page, and open the next video.

31

```
<!DOCTYPE HTML>
<HTML>
    <HEAD>
        ELI OVER EASY
    </HEAD>
    <BODY>
        <P>I MISS YOU</P>
    </BODY>
</HTML>
```

On today's episode of Renee's Test Kitchen, *I have a very special surprise for all of you. Today, you get to see the man behind the camera, my producer, my own sous chef, and my husband, James Adams.*

Dad crosses into the frame and blushes in embarrassment. Something about seeing them interact in our old kitchen, in our old Minnesota home, makes my heart ache. They have some silly, probably scripted banter, and it's wild to see the differences between them. Now on her sixth episode, Mom's completely comfortable behind the camera, but Dad seems almost paralyzed by fear. Even though he knows this is going on a private YouTube channel? I can't help but smile as he fumbles through his introduction.

Right. So! I'm James, and I'm, um . . . so excited to be a special guest on Renee's Test Kitchen. *I've, uh, been a fan for a long time.*

They laugh, and it seems to thaw his frozen body language.

Anyway, okay. So, I want to teach you one of my favorite recipes to make: chicken fajitas.

I cover my face with my hand. Well. That explains why he was so weird about offering to cook fajitas that night. He was doing it to catch me in my lie, but I hadn't even gotten to the episode yet!

But I think back to that day, and we had so much fun. Even if it was supposed to just call me out on my lies, it ended up being an awesome experience.

In the video, Mom does all the prep with the veggies while Dad lists the ingredients and starts prepping the chicken. He cuts the chicken breast into strips, then seasons them heavily with the same mix that we used during our cooking session. He knows everything by heart, so it's another one of those recipes where he just says "a handful of chili powder, a dash of cumin, a pinch of cayenne pepper."

I love these two, but they need to learn how to give more precise measurements. I roll my eyes, and Mom takes over the narration as Dad starts the process.

My dearest James is tossing the spices, chicken strips, and a heavy pour of vegetable oil in a bowl, and he's using a grill pan to get nice grill marks on them. You can use a cast-iron skillet, a nonstick pan, a grill—if it's not negative ten degrees outside, like it is now here in Minneapolis!—however you like to cook the chicken, just be careful. They cook pretty quickly when they're in strips.

Meanwhile, Mom decides to make her own Mexican-flavored rice from scratch and warms up a can of refried beans.

You could make them yourself, but who has the time?!

As you can see, James is juggling a lot of things
right now, which is why I always say if you have
someone else who can help out . . . it makes it a lot
easier.

She gives him a sweet smile.

But I guess that's true for most things.

My eyes are flooded with tears, but I don't feel
quite as hopeless and sad as I'd expect. It's refreshing,
nostalgic, and sweet. My life got so uprooted when
we moved to New York City, and a part of me hates
that Mom's going to miss so much of my life. But she
was really happy doing what she was doing, and I
hold on to that.

Mom cuts back to the camera while Dad gets a solid
char on all the veggies.

I like to serve them with corn tortillas, but
my husband and son like flour. We're both very
stubborn about this. So instead of fighting about it,
we buy both. Since we're getting close to finishing,

*I'm going to set up all the toppings and throw the
tortillas on the grill to get them nice and warm for
our meal.*

The video starts to wrap up as they set up a whole
fajita bar on our kitchen table. The camera pans across
the table, and suddenly I hear a younger version of my
voice cut through.

*When's dinner gonna be ready? And what's Dad
doing with his phone?*

Mom laughs.

*Oh, he's just taking video evidence of this feast
we're about to eat. Go wash up, and we'll be ready
in five.*

Dad holds the camera up so he and Mom are in the
screen. He speaks.

Well, thanks for joining us for another episode of
Renee's Test Kitchen. *Happy eating!*

I shut the laptop, and without thinking about it, I start crying. Tears of . . . something—not quite joy, not quite pain—fall down my face. On cue, Dad peeks in the door and, seeing my state, comes over and puts his arm around me.

"I can't watch that one," he says. "I can watch every other one, and I have—so many times—but that one is just too much for me."

I wipe a few tears from my eyes and give a fake chuckle. "Can't imagine why."

Just then, the doorbell rings.

"Probably just Mat," I say and jump up, blotting my eyes with a tissue to get rid of any residual tears. I walk through the apartment with Dad following a few paces behind me. But when I get to the door, I hear a *very* different voice on the other side.

"Your surprise has arrived," Dad says.

I open the door, and all I see is a flash of stark black hair as Riley tackles me with a hug. My cousin, and my aunt, have come to the city.

Dad's Fajitas

INGREDIENTS

Flour tortillas (or corn if you're like mom)

2 tbsp vegetable oil

2 bell peppers (1 red and 1 green . . . plus a
yellow one if Ann insists!)

2 onions

1 lb chicken, cut into strips (Dad takes care of
this . . . I'm still iffy on touching raw meat)

1 store-bought fajita seasoning packet (plus some
extra cayenne!)

The best part: TOPPINGS (Avocado, Cheese,
Sour Cream, Cilantro, Limes to squeeze on top!)

DIRECTIONS

In a big bowl, toss the chicken strips with the oil
and half the seasoning packet

Heat a little bit of oil in a big skillet over

medium-high, once hot, toss in the veggies, the
rest of the seasoning packet, a half-cup of
water, and stir

Toss in chicken and stir until chicken is cooked
through (I'm letting Dad take care of
that one so I don't make everyone sick with
undercooked chicken)

Serve with tortillas and alllllllll the beautiful
toppings

CHEF'S TIP: If you have someone else who
can help out . . . it makes it a lot easier.

32

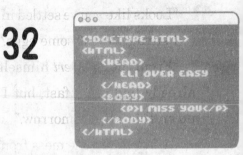

After we dust ourselves off from Riley's overeager tackling incident, I give Aunt Chloe a big hug too. I haven't seen her since Mom's funeral, and I'd forgotten how much I missed having them around.

"Is this why you're on a 'mental health hiatus' from streaming this week?" I ask. "You're such a liar!"

She shrugs. "I couldn't ruin the surprise. Uncle James has been planning this for weeks!"

I turn to Dad. "You have?"

"Yep!" He gives a proud smile. "I thought we could both use some family time, and Aunt Chloe kept saying how she wanted to visit the city."

"Riley's never been!" my aunt says. "I only visited that one time right after Renee moved."

She looks at all the mess from our breakfast, and at our equally messy living room.

"Looks like you've settled in," Riley says sarcastically.

I shrug. "Want some eggs?"

"From the *eggspert* himself?" Riley fake gasps. "We already had breakfast, but I will definitely take you up on that offer tomorrow."

As I clean up the mess from breakfast, Dad gets the apartment set up for guests—Aunt Chloe is going to stay in my room, while Riley and I will sleep on the pullout couch. Just like our old slumber parties in Minnesota.

"I am amped up," Riley says. "Should we go explore the city?"

I look to Dad, who gives me a nod. "Let's all go. Do you want to invite Mat?"

"Ooh, Mat. To be honest, he's half the reason I wanted to come." Riley nudges me.

"Hey!" I snap.

But then she adds, "Well, you were the other half."

It takes us about thirty minutes to finish getting settled. I change clothes, and we meet Mat outside the building. I make the introductions, and then Dad turns to me.

"Where do you want to go?" he asks. "I have tickets

to bigger things this week, so maybe something low-key today, since they just traveled. Maybe a park?"

I look to Mat, and he gives me a nod. "I know just the place."

The adults follow behind us while Riley, Mat, and I all catch up.

"Eli's got me hooked on your streams," Mat says. "They're so funny."

"Thank you, thank you." She sighs dramatically. "It's not always easy being a niche internet microcelebrity, but I do love my fans."

I laugh. "How do you stay so modest?"

"It's a gift." She shrugs. "I packed my ring light, by the way, so I think we need to get *Eli's Test Kitchen* up and running this week."

"Yes! That's what I've been telling him to do!" Mat says.

I blush, but there's a hint of excitement there too. With Mat and Riley by my side, I feel like I can do anything.

Mat and I walk briskly, and Riley struggles to keep up, so we slow down to a more Midwestern pace. We walk across large avenues and push our way through crowds of people, all to get to our final destination: Greenwich Village.

"I love this city so much," Riley says. "Maybe I'll move here someday. And it's not even the city itself but how it kind of changes you. You seem so confident now. Your dad told my mom that you'd started to put down roots here, and I believe it."

"He said that?" I ask. "Huh. Well, I think we're going to end up coming back soon anyway."

"No!" She gasps. "I mean, I would love to see you more, but I really wanted to brag about my cosmopolitan cousin at school this year."

I shrug. "Nothing I can do."

"Blech. Parents."

Mat and I make knowing eye contact.

As we walk, the skyscrapers start shrinking, the large office buildings fade into brick apartment buildings, and a feeling of calm sweeps over the neighborhood. Pride flags hang all around, and I feel Mat drift a little closer. He looks to me and tilts his head.

A question. One I know the answer to.

I grab his hand, firmly, and we lace our fingers together. We meander around the neighborhood until we find the park outside Stonewall, and the five of us take up two benches next to each other. Birds chirp, passersby talk in quiet hums, and with Mat's hand still in mine, I feel peace for the first time in ages.

"I don't want to leave here," I tell Riley and Mat. "I wish we had more time."

I don't really know if "we" means me and Dad, or me and Mat. Probably both.

"I'm sorry, cuz," Riley says. "This city is special."

"Very special," Mat echoes.

33

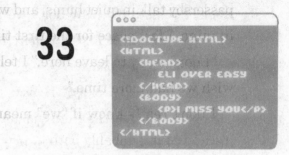

```
<!DOCTYPE HTML>
<HTML>
    <HEAD>
        ELI OVER EASY
    </HEAD>
    <BODY>
        <P>I MISS YOU</P>
    </BODY>
</HTML>
```

The next day, Dad takes me, Riley, and Aunt Chloe around to see some of the bigger tourist attractions: Times Square and Rockefeller Plaza (specifically, the M&M's store for me and the Nintendo store for Riley), One World Trade, and we even take a boat out to Ellis Island and the Statue of Liberty.

We get back around three in the afternoon, and we're all sore and dehydrated. We take turns showering and chugging water, and the conversation turns to dinner.

"I have an idea," Riley says. "What if . . . Eli cooks and I stream it? We can set you up with your own account, but if you stream from mine, you can get some of my followers. I can take care of all the tech!"

I feel the heat go straight to my cheeks. "What would

I cook? Something new?"

"That would be cool." Dad thinks about it. "What about . . . actually, why don't we all watch the final episode of *Renee's Test Kitchen*? I remember ending with a big crowd-pleaser."

"Are you sure it's okay?" I say as I open up my laptop. He nods, so I cast the final video to our TV.

Fresh from her shower, Aunt Chloe gasps when she sees her sister on the screen.

"I totally forgot about these videos!" she says. "She would have made a great TV chef, I truly think so. She's so genuine."

I nod. "Here goes nothing."

Hello, and welcome to the final episode of the first season of Renee's Test Kitchen. *I'd gone back and forth about what to do for this episode. Something ultra-fancy? Something elaborate and fussy?*

But then I sat back and thought, You know what I really love to make? Deep-dish pizza. *The restaurant I worked at was right next to this amazing Chicago-style deep-dish pizza place, and I ate there all the time, eventually becoming friends with the owners and getting tips on how to make it myself.*

For my deep-dish pizza, you'll need a cast-iron skillet. This is what gets the crust all golden and crispy. I'll also go through all the ingredients, which I have all prepped thanks to my sous chef.

She winks to Dad behind the camera.

Aunt Chloe reaches over Riley to grab a tissue. It can't be easy for her, or for any of us, to watch Mom like this. So happy, so excited, having no idea how little time she had left. But maybe that's okay. If she knew, would she have done anything different? I highly doubt it.

This recipe, unlike some of my others, is really forgiving. You can make mistakes—hey, everyone makes mistakes—you can screw things up, but in the end, it'll all turn out the way it's supposed to. Which is, you know, delicious. Even bad pizza is pizza!

She mixes the dough in her stand mixer, and over time, the camera makes a few cuts to show the dough rising. Eventually, she takes out her skillet, pours a heavy amount of oil into it, and presses the dough in

259

before layering all the ingredients—cheese first!—and popping it in the oven.

I don't take many notes because I know this is the last video. I can't look away. I know, after this, I'll be on my own in my journey. My cooking journey, that is. Eventually, the video ends, and we all sit around in a comfortable silence.

"I think it's the perfect recipe," I say. "And it'll be *full* of chances to make a fool out of myself. I'm in."

"Chloe, want to come shop with me?" Dad asks. "And Eli, make sure you invite Mat over. Mrs. Martinez too. We have two cast-iron skillets, and I think we should put them both to use!"

"Are you ready?" Mat asks.

He's sitting on a bar stool behind Riley's ring light, waiting for us to give him the go-ahead to start streaming. The stream name Riley chose, "Surprise Stream! Debuting Eli's Test Kitchen !cooking! fails" doesn't give me a ton of confidence, but I'm glad that for my first-ever stream, I'm doing it with a pro.

Riley gives me an encouraging smile, and I give the go-ahead to Mat. He starts the stream, and she starts welcoming everyone. She uses my phone to join the stream and see who of her followers are joining, so she can give personalized hellos to people.

I just stand awkwardly in the frame, feeling my heart rate double.

Hi, everyone! I've got something really special for you today. You know how I said I'd be taking a hiatus this week? Well, that was a lie. But it was a lie for a good cause! I'm with my cousin Eli, who you can follow over at the handle ElisTestKitchen, all one word. He's a brand-new streamer who's going to bring you into his life as an amateur cook. And today, we're making Chicago-style deep-dish pizzas, so you're going to want to stick around. Eli, over to you.

Um, hey! I've been a longtime watcher of Riley's streams, but this is the first time I've ever tried something like this on my own. So I hope it works out. And . . . if it doesn't . . . well, I guess that'll be some good content?

Riley shows me the stream chat, and between the dozens of clapping-hands emojis, I see comments like

"You can do it!" A confidence grows in me that takes me by surprise. Riley's community is so special—if you excuse the odd troll or two—and having forty-six strangers cheering me on feels so empowering.

I think about how Mom would have loved seeing this, and instinctively flinch, waiting for the tears to come—but this time, I just feel happy and proud.

We start by making the dough. Riley injects personality into all of my instructions, making cheeky jokes or quick remarks, responding to people in the chat. Meanwhile, I carefully mix the flour, cornmeal, salt, sugar, and yeast into the bowl of Mom's stand mixer. I switch to the dough-hook attachment and start the mixer.

Now we mix in the water. It's important to use warm water here, because that's what activates the yeast and makes the crust rise. You also want to pour it in slowly here, so it doesn't splatter.

My nerves get the best of me, and I dump too much of the water in at one time, and a cloud of flour puffs up in my face. I cough while Riley cracks up.

Or . . . I'll just dump it all in and get flour
everywhere. That's fine.

The chat lights up, but it's nothing too negative.
Now there are seventy-five people watching live, and
the viewer count keeps climbing! Once the dough is
mixed, I drop it into a clear bowl with a little bit of
oil, cover it with cling wrap, and explain that it needs
to sit for an hour.

Thankfully, my cuz Eli thought ahead, because
he already has one ball of dough all proofed and
ready! While we make the first pizza, we'll let the
second pizza dough rise and then swap it out once
they're all done.

I plop the proofed dough into a well-oiled cast-iron
skillet, and I start pressing the dough to the sides.

You want this to be pretty thin. Remember, it's
going to rise while it bakes too, and you don't want
a weird ratio of sauce to cheese. The skillet and

the oil are crucial—it's almost like you're deep-
frying the crust, which is what gives it that golden,
crunchy, perfect texture.

Riley and I assemble the first pizza and throw it in the oven, and while we wait for that to bake, she chats with a few commenters. She lets me pitch my new cookie web app and drop the link in the chat. Dozens of people start commenting, saying how cool it looks and that they're bookmarking it.

I make eye contact with Mat, who's just smiling behind the camera. I smile back, and blush when I realize I just did that on a live stream that's pushing three hundred viewers.

Over the course of an hour, we're able to pull out the first pizza and place the second one in the oven. Mat comes over with the phone to shoot the pizza from all angles and cause about a hundred commenters to spam the chat with pizza emojis.

"Is that a good thing?" I ask Riley.

"It's a good thing." She laughs. "Also, I don't want to startle you, but you already have eighty-five followers on your new account, so people are loving this content. I told you!"

After the pizza cools, I cut a slice for Riley to eat on camera. She exaggerates how good it is, to put on a performance for her fans—and to get optimum FOMO—but I appreciate it anyway.

I come in and take a bite too, but once the crispy fried crust, tangy sauce, and gooey cheese hits my tongue, I realize . . . maybe she's not exaggerating.

All right, this is Eli's Test Kitchen, *signing off for the day. I'll be streaming on my own page soon, so if you haven't already, make sure to follow me over at ElisTestKitchen, all one word.*

Riley takes over and gives her followers a proper sign-off, then the six of us—me, Dad, Aunt Chloe, Riley, Mat, and Mrs. Martinez—all sit in the living room devouring our freshly made pizza.

Mom's Deep-Dish Pizza

INGREDIENTS

For the pizza crust:

3 cups flour

Cornmeal

Salt

1 packet of instant yeast

1 tbsp sugar> This is basically a science experiment!!

1 cup of warm water (more if it's too dry!)

Olive oil to coat the bowl while the dough rises

Toppings:

Tomato Sauce ... See Mom's "Perfect Pasta Sauce" recipe

**use that leftover sauce that we froze

Mozzarella cheese (a whole bag per pizza)

Parmesan cheese (basically as much cheese as you can handle)

DIRECTIONS

For the dough: Combine all the dry ingredients in a stand mixer with a dough hook, then add warm water.

This is when the science happens!!! The yeast gets activated by the warm water, eats the sugar, and makes the whole thing rise! NOTE: Eli, try not to geek out too much on the stream!

Beat the dough for 4-5 minutes, until it all starts to come together. (Mom says you can add more water or more flour if it's too dry or too sticky!)

Form the dough into a ball and put it in a big bowl with olive oil to coat it. Cover, and let rise for one hour until it doubles in size!

Plop the dough on a lightly floured counter, roll it out, and get all your other ingredients together.

****PREHEAT OVEN NOW ELI****

Smoosh the dough into a heavily oiled cast-iron skillet, then layer the toppings CHEESE FIRST (this keeps the sauce from getting the crust all soggy) then top with tomato sauce and powdered parm.

Bake for 25-30 minutes (Mom said 25, but mine took 30, so maybe our ovens are different?)

USE AN OVEN MITT to remove the pan and let sit for 15 minutes while trying not to drool everywhere. Cut it up and dig in!

CHEF'S TIP: You can make mistakes—hey, everyone makes mistakes—you can screw things up, but in the end, it'll all turn out the way it's supposed to.

<!DOCTYPE HTML>
<HTML>
  <HEAD>
    ELI OVER EASY
  </HEAD>
  <BODY>
    <P>I MISS YOU</P>
  </BODY>
</HTML>

34

O n Wednesday, Riley and Aunt Chloe start packing up to go back. They're visiting some family friends in Philly before ultimately returning to Minnesota. My heart aches to be saying goodbye to them, the only family I've seen in months, but we really made the most of this trip.

"Eli, if you ever need me, I'm here. Okay? Whether you need streaming tips or a shoulder to cry on or anything. I'm your big cousin, and I've gotta look out for you. Got it?"

"I'm there for you too. Whether you need to vent to me or you need someone to drive those trolls out of your chat, I'm here—I promise."

I hug her and Aunt Chloe goodbye, and as they leave,

Dad puts his arm around me.

"So, was it a good surprise?" he asks.

"The best."

"I do have another surprise. But this one . . . I'm not sure how you're going to like it."

We walk over to the couch and take our seats, and I give him a concerned look. A feeling of dread bubbles up within me because I know what he's going to say.

"I got that job," he says. I keep my face neutral. "I'll be full-time remote again in just over two weeks. Which is bad news for you because—"

"I know, I know." I sigh. "I know we're moving back to Minnesota. You're right, it makes sense. I'm really happy you got the job you wanted."

He clears his throat. "It's bad news for you because I'm going to be around the apartment all the time again."

I give him a confused look, and he returns it with one of his own.

"When this summer started, I wanted nothing more than to get out of Manhattan. I hated the noise, the people, the traffic, the weather, the cramped space. Mom's death made me so anxious to be out in public, I was wearing two masks every time I was on the subway . . . I was being ridiculous.

"But something happened recently. When I walked around with you, and you knew the bodega owner, the lady who runs the veggie cart, all the corner-store employees. When you took us to that park outside Stonewall, and you just stared at the waving flags holding Mat's hand . . . I realized that *you* gave this city a chance, and it paid off."

"But don't we have to get back?"

"Remote work means I can work from anywhere," he says plainly. "And look, our lease isn't up for another few months. Let's give it our all while we're here. And if we like it, we stay. If we don't, we go." He smiles. "But I think we'll like it."

A smile comes across my face, and I wrap him in a big hug. "I think so too!"

Immediately, I want to tell Mat. But . . . that just makes me sad because Mat's supposed to be leaving, *today*. I send him a quick text to see if he's around, then step outside to go knock on Mrs. Martinez's apartment door.

Before I can do that, he opens it.

"Hi, Mat."

"Eli."

"I wanted to let you know that Dad and I are staying

here, for a while at least. So we'll be here with Mrs. Martinez. I promise, I'll watch out for her as much as I can. I promise, okay? You don't have to worry at all. And maybe when you come visit, we can still see each other and cook together. What do you think?"

He looks at me tentatively and says, "I think I want to give you a kiss."

My cheeks flush with heat. "Oh? Oh wow. Okay."

I close my eyes, because that seems like the right thing to do, but I open them back up when he laughs.

"Sorry, I don't know what I'm doing!" I shout.

He crosses toward me and gives me a small peck on the lips, which makes my whole body tingle.

"Neither do I," he says. "Thank you for offering to help Grandma out, but you don't need to. I was coming over to tell you that *we* are staying. Mom's moving in to help out and get Grandma back on her feet a bit until we find a new place. Now that she's . . . single . . . she said she wants to try living in the city. So we might find an apartment of our own here, if we can find the right one."

"I'm really sorry your parents are splitting up," I say, trying to tamp down how excited I am to know he's not going to be leaving. That he'll be next door for a while, and maybe he'll be close by for a long time.

"It's okay," he says, though his face seems a little twisted. Recovering from that kind of grief must take a long time.

"Whenever it gets hard, just know . . . I'll be right here. You helped me through so much: pulling off all my cooking attempts, making me laugh when I was sad . . ."

"Eating four hundred eggs," he says.

I shudder. "You're a trooper."

He laughs, and I pull him into the biggest, most Midwestern hug I can manage. We might not have forever, but we have a little more time. And for once, that's more than enough for me.

35

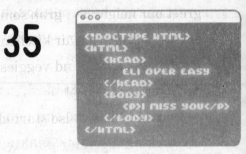

```
<!DOCTYPE HTML>
<HTML>
    <HEAD>
        ELI OVER EASY
    </HEAD>
    <BODY>
        <P>I MISS YOU</P>
    </BODY>
</HTML>
```

A few weeks later, I soak up my last days of sleeping in before school starts.

Every morning, I make breakfast for me and Dad. Sometimes breakfast burritos, sometimes eggs Benedict—though I still hate poaching eggs—sometimes scrambled eggs, and sometimes we still get bagels from Hank's—hey, I can't cook every day.

I stream my videos at night, only a couple times a week, and I've gotten almost a thousand followers already. I've been pivoting more to tips, and went through a whole egg tutorial without setting the fire alarm off even once.

Dad's getting settled into his new job, and he's

274

more than thrilled to be working remotely. Every day for lunch, we'll take a walk around the block, just to greet our neighbors, grab some snacks at the bodega, or chat with Ann. Our kitchen is stocked with some of the biggest fruits and veggies because of her, but we can't get her to stop!

Dad and I have also started seeing therapists, and we're slowly opening up more about our grief. Some days are hard, some days feel easy, but either way, we're working on it. This morning is a little hard, so before I get out of bed, I start rewatching one of Mom's old videos.

"Hey, buddy." Dad pops his head into my room. "Thought I heard Renee's voice. You doing okay?"

"Yeah," I say. "Just missing her today. I feel like I've changed so much this summer, and I wish I still had her with me to talk to about everything . . . or even just give me advice."

Dad laughs. "She's given you plenty of advice."

"What do you mean?"

"You should take another look at that notebook you put all those recipes in."

He shuts the door, and I pause the video. I don't

know what he's talking about, but I scramble over to my notebook and start flipping through all of the recipes I wrote in there. Recipes from Mom, Dad, and Mrs. Martinez fill the pages, but one thing stands out to me: the chef's tip at the bottom of each page:

You can't do something perfectly until you've

messed it up every way possible first.

Take it low and slow. You're in no rush.

When things get too stressful, just breathe . . .

and get your bearings. When you're ready . . .

keep moving forward.

It doesn't have to be perfect.

Like Great-Granny says, "Trust your heart."

. . . sometimes it takes a little pain to find the joy.

Cooking with someone, or cooking for someone, is

the best way to make someone feel better.

If you have someone else who can help out . . .

it makes it a lot easier.

You can make mistakes—hey, everyone makes

mistakes—you can screw things up, but in the end, it'll all turn out the way it's supposed to. It's okay if it takes a little longer than you were hoping.

I close the notebook and hold it to my chest, and smile, because I know I have plenty of advice that'll last me the rest of my life.

EPILOGUE

Eli's Test Kitchen—Episode 5

Is this working? Hello? Can you see me okay? All right, looking at the comments it seems like . . . yep, Riley says everything is working. So I guess I'll just dive in.

Hi, everyone! I'm Eli Adams, and welcome to another round of Eli's Test Kitchen. *My mom always says that with a little bit of practice, and a whole lot of heart, anyone can be a chef . . . and I'm going to try to prove that again today. If you like what I'm doing, feel free to hype it up in chat, throw in some emotes, and subscribe.*

. . . Did I say that right? I'm still kinda learning the terminology on here. Okay, so I know a lot of

278

you came here from my cousin Riley's streams, but be forewarned: I am still pretty new at streaming. But one thing I've learned over this summer is that I am a good cook. And a good coder—check the link in my bio to view my free Perfect Cookie Recipe web app!

I usually cook from this notebook right here, which is a mess of scribbled notes taken from the advice of my mom, my dad, my friend Mathias— who's just off screen, waiting to taste-test—plus his grandma and basically anyone else around me who can cook.

But today, I wanted to show you a dish that doesn't need much of a recipe. I never really knew what cooking from the heart meant when my mom said it, and to be honest I still don't, but maybe we'll all figure it out together along the way.

All right. Dad, you ready to handle the camera? Riley, you good to moderate the chat? Mat, you ready to fan the fire alarm if it goes off?

I'll take your laughter as a yes. Okay, I think we're all set!

If you're just joining us, this is Eli's Test Kitchen, *episode five: a simple breakfast hash topped with the perfect over-easy egg.*

Let's get started!

ACKNOWLEDGMENTS

As always, some thank-yous are in order:

To my agent, Brent Taylor. You first offered to represent me and my career six years ago (to the day, as I write this!), and your enthusiasm for my projects has never waned since. I can't imagine navigating this career without your keen guidance and never-ending support.

To my fantastic editor, Megan Ilnitzki. You really got Eli's character and story from the very first pitch—with you, I always know my books are in good hands. Also, to my entire team at Harper for all their work to put this book in the hands of readers everywhere: Mark Rifkin, Shona McCarthy, Emily Mannon, Patty Rosati, Mimi Rankin, Andrea Pappenheimer, Kristen

Eckhardt, and Anna Ravenelle.

To Violet Tobacco for bringing your brilliant use of color and light to portray Eli's journey—and his grief—with your touching cover illustration, and to Amy Ryan and Kathy Lam for the incredible jacket design.

To all the librarians, teachers, booksellers, and reviewers who have supported my career through my six published books. You've welcomed me into the children's space so warmly, and you've fought for my books every step of the away—despite this challenging climate—to help protect and support queer kids and teens. You're all the real heroes here!

And to all my readers: Whether this is the first book of mine that you've read or you've read them all, thank you so much for helping me live out this absolute dream of a career. Getting to put stories of queer joy, acceptance, and excellence out in the world for the people who need it most has been an honor. Again, thank you for being with me on this amazing ride.